THE JAMAICA KOLLECTION
OF THE SHANTE DREAM ARKIVE

T0357299

Also by Marcia Douglas
FROM NEW DIRECTIONS

The Marvellous Equations of the Dread

Marcia Douglas

THE JAMAICA KOLLECTION
OF THE SHANTE DREAM ARKIVE

being dreamity, algoriddims, chants & riffs

A NEW DIRECTIONS PAPERBOOK ORIGINAL

Manufactured in the United States of America
First published as a New Directions Paperbook Original (NDP1627) in 2025

Library of Congress Cataloging-in-Publication Data
Names: Douglas, Marcia, author.
Title: The Jamaica Kollection of the Shante Dream Arkive:
being dreamity, algoriddims, chants & riffs / Marcia Douglas.
Description: First edition. | New York : New Directions Publishing, 2025.
Identifiers: LCCN 2024026062 | ISBN 9780811231176 (paperback)
| ISBN 9780811239264 (ebook)
Subjects: LCGFT: Poetry. | Short stories.
Classification: LCC PS3554.O8274 J36 2025 | DDC 811/.54--dc23/eng/20240614

2   4   6   8   10   9   7   5   3   1

New Directions Books are published for James Laughlin
by New Directions Publishing Corporation
80 Eighth Avenue, New York, New York 10011

FROM THE ARKIVE

for Avani

All I know is, the edge of the world is a betting shop in Papine. Horses sometimes leap there, and so do men and women. Nobody knows where they disappear after that, but I think they end up in a place swirling with stars, cinnamon and brown sugar; yellow cornmeal sprinkling their skin. A man with four plaits curled up at the ends, meets them halfway; he kisses their foot-bottom with his starapple mouth. I would like to go to that place.

—CARMEN INNOCENCIA

Mama! You can hear me now? I sound like a swallowtail butterfly, Mama. Did you know they are the largest butterflies in Jamaica? And they are almost extinct. I read it in a book. —ANJAHLA

> *I've always been interested in interrogating the "novel" as a form and exploring what else that genre might become, particularly within a Caribbean context. In the Caribbean we are adept at making and re-making—we see this in how European language and African linguistic memory become "nation language," or in how R&B and gospel and West African drumming become reggae, and there are many more examples. Given this history of innovation, I find myself interested in pushing at the boundaries of what it means to write a Caribbean novel and have taken this on as an ongoing creative quest.*
>
> —The author, interviewed by Dr. Carole Boyce Davies in *Praxis*

And hear this: Something there is about a good reggae rewind and the way it interrupts a chune and takes us back—just so we won't forget; let me say that again.

And also this: as a child I was mesmerized by my grandma's old-time Jamaican country house—the walls flour-pasted with photos, bits of newspaper, old calendars and any "pretty paper" she could find. I didn't fully realise it then, but now that I think of it, that wall marked me and was an early apprenticeship—my first understanding of how stories layer or how they connect and disconnect. I still remember myself—a small girl—looking at that wall, the way one might gaze at the sea, or night sky. Did grandma's pitchy-patchy tire evil spirits and make them run? That humble house was my first teacher.

Years later and I still stand in wonda of how our stories layer and of where and how we come to find them. From book to book, I've been conscious of testing the possibilities of narrative and questioning notions of what a "novel" is or how I, as an Afro-Caribbean woman, might engage with it. *The Jamaica Kollection of the Shante Dream Arkive* continues my exploration of how the chaos and riddim of Caribbean rebel space works. Re-thinking genre, and also, resisting genre, this is a project about Caribbean migration and fugitivity, and the relentless ways in which stories and species change and transform; disappear and return; collide and mash up and rise up. To recover such a story is to journey deep into an arkive of dream, memory and imagination and participate in a collective healing. Along the way, the novelist finds refuge and succour in the poet's house; and the poet finds refuge and succour in the novelist's, co-creating across genres and herstories and chants and riffs; invoking ancestors; excavating voices; charting new cosmologies; leaping out of established ways of telling. The terrain is treacherous—the writer writes like an outlaw and the reader is invited to read like one too.

—MD

THE JAMAICA KOLLECTION
OF THE SHANTE DREAM ARKIVE

*kurata;**

For years, you kept your milk teeth in a tin. Then later,
there were the small white bones you found under
a tamarind tree—maybe a bird's? Years, and still you
have your mother's knife—the one she cut cake with
on her wedding day, your father's hand over hers; and
too, you have that tiny scrap of blue—linoleum from
the old floor of your grandmother's house. Kuration is
a life-long calling, the recovery of secrets and bottomless riddim tings—artifakts with no density or form.

Ships come and go in Kingston harbour, and there are
things you discern on the seafloor—bits of ancestor
bone; and an old monocle for watching the soon-come
shore; and here, some left-over grief from the disappeared—

For what if one day we forget coral reef? There are
seeds and pods in your collection, so old, they deserve
wi nuff-respect. And as you record the alignment of
stars and galaxies with the precise moment of ripe-&-
drop, it occurs to you that space-time and mango-time
are one and the same.

You reason all this, standing in a doorway, listening for
the ancestor and eating No. 11.

---

* **kurata:** *the keeper of lists in the house of dread; aka, ms. ellaineous*
  close synonym: **selecta** *(as in,* wheel it up one more time*); also:* **DJ**
  *early 18th C.: one who gathers flora, fauna, people and objects to kurate escape; one
who communes with modda earth; one who maps the stars.*
  *21st C.: one who gathers flora, fauna, people, objects and stories in resistance to col-
lective amnesia; one who loves our modda and seeks to conserve her; one who charts
quantum riddim.*

3

GENUINE HERSTORY

/truth is,
there is no such thing as a beginning—

But there is always hurricane in it; always. They say, there was a time the ancestor, Quaco, dipped and whirled to a place of flightless birds. He rode a spiraling ting filled with salt-wata tears and cane blossom; turnin-turnin;

and another time, a sista rode a vinyl record in her dream to a place of no gravity, only space junk, hoof reverb and libation of again-again.

Red and white hibiscus flowers open and close—wheel their skirts in the spirit—and they say,

millions of years ago, the *Xenothrix* monkey arrived at this salt-&-sugar island, twirling on a drift-log raft. The log—spat into the sea from the storm mouth of a river—was rot and cedar. Not much is known about the journey, but according to some, there were two travelers—scared and wet-furred, they hunkered down in a hollow of the wood, and rode the waves all the way from South America to a stretch of quiet, brown-sand beach, where washed ashore, they slept for a whole day, egret and pelican walking curious-beaked around them.

The *Xenothrix* were among the first to wheel-&-come here; though later, there were others—sea-faring seed pods, rice rodents, and little brown anole lizards—flora-fauna folk who crossed sea, driven by wind and rain and the call of story. Back then, the island had no name. And how beautiful she was in her no-nameness; colonized only by little humming and flying tings which flitted in her soon 600 species of dread-fern.

And there were other travelers too—monk seals. From how far, and for how long, did those *Monachus* swim to find these shores? They barked sea riddim psalm, all oneness and meditation with the big seas. Each made the alone journey; now-&-then gulls hitching a ride when they surfaced above salt wata.

But, *Caracara tellustris* may have been here even longer. Family to flightless falcons, they preferred walking and chasing fiddler crabs, having pre-gifted their flight feathers—to Africans in the yet-to-come who would need to return to their ancestral land. Imagine that. It takes the evolution of a whole species to help accomplish such a feat.

The humans, well, they came in dug-out canoes—skimming the exposed rim of South America, then following current—taking the path of *Xenothrix* pioneers. They carried left-over leaves, red roots and yellow grain; a woman carried forget-mi-not DNA; a young girl brought a pet snail. How relieved canoe-people were to see this land. The monk seals on the beach—we now call Hellshire—greeted them. The *Xenothrix* watched from the trees.

Cara-cara-cara-cara was the sound a bird made.

Some say, a fossil of a *Xenothrix* was found many years come-later, 1920— in Pickney Mama Cave in the Cockpit Country of Jamaica. From there it went to a wooden cabinet in the American Museum of Natural History. And some say, *Monachus*'s sad dark eyes were last sighted in the Caribbean Sea in 1952. Her skin and hair have been stored away in a forgetting room in a cold and far country. *Caracara tellustris* fossils have been found in Skeleton Cave on the southern part of the island. They are presently in a bottom drawer in a university museum. *Cara-cara-cara-cara* is what stars chant when they fly. Scientists are keen to discover more—

(But the thing is, certain artifakts are arkived only in that fissure between sleep and dead, dream and just-wake—

a 1494 milk tooth can be found afloat in that space; and a cough on board the *Henrietta Marie*; the lost foot of a slave-girl's shoe is there too—running from beat-up, she was; and-look, railroad tracks to that place you can never reach; and there-so: mistress's wedding veil 5,280 feet long; and passports, ship logs, flight feathers, boarding passes to countries of she-magination; mind the door that swings open and shut, waiting for you to slip through to a place of riva run, cliff leap, and woman wail—

in this blue-blue between there are 562 species of snails, and chips of kitchen conversation that could change the course of history; *a morsel of genuine*, they float like *herstory*; here, a letter with a last Kingston buttercup pressed inside; *is a thing so rare*; silver buttons from deep sea bottom; *as to be always valuable*; a small see-through envelope of 1839 ganja seeds; and a shoe box of phalanges and metatarsals; a jar of wild-hog breast milk waits here; a scandal bag tied tight with a double knot; a woman at U.S. customs; a cassette tape of running feet; a small, close-knit family of two hundred year-old fruit flies thrive in this between; and one solitary own-self sugar ant that played a part in the Morant Bay Rebellion; Ms. Zora's camera is here; and oi, unidentified epiphyte [#146]; and baby Quaco's navel string, of course; but look-here—a sealed box of truth, and another of lies; and instructions for mixing two together, so you can tell it right.)

In hurri/cane time/ galaxies spin, but not the same direction all/ story twists like a double helix/beetles roll their dung into balls; tur/nin birds fly in spiral as they holl/ah and pray/wheel it up &

Entah when yu ready—

The way in all bramble and wait-a-bit, wards off evil; red crotons set in water rest in the corners, and look: atoms of runaway slaves spin in empty rum bottles—the bottle-glass dark, almost black, and with no label. Centuries later, there is still Old Plantation scent and a whole story inside.

Keep going and find that epiphyte [item #146]—a discrete plant, currently unknown to science. A very emotive individual, it reveals itself—on occasion—to runaways, fugitives and motherless kin. Like all epiphytes, #146 longs to be with others and loves deeply.

But first; watch-here, buried deep—the photos from Ms. Z's Kodak

Junior Six-16, the exposures hidden in a cardboard box in an undisclosed space. Beware. If someone knows, it will make news. Oh-the-scholars. Oh-the-estate-keepers. Oh-the-Museums-of-Everything. They will descend like a flock; the grapefruit tree in the front yard will shiver and lose all its leaves.

THAT FISSURE BETWEEN

Exposure I [recovered film from Kodak Junior Six-16]

Check this: Ms. Z. lost her beautiful black camera in 1936 while on a Jamaica Guggenheim Fellowship and out hiking with Accompong maroons, descendants of a 17th century Cockpit Country runaway band. In the 17th century they ran zig-zag through the hills—the way lizards move. Forward to 1936 and here they are in black & white film hunting wild hog with Ms. Z. Leave it to Ms. Z. to convince someone to hunt hog in the treacherous limestone of the Cockpit. While here, check out the camera lens attached to bellows which fold in and out like accordion lungs. Ms. Z's lungs; breathing, deep and long. Eight 2 1/2 × 4 1/4 exposures on number 616 roll film.

The Kodak was found in November, 1937 by Laverne Downs, a young girl running from home. By then, Ms. Z. was long-gone, having left for Haiti, then the U.S. The camera was discovered lodged between rocks; everything intact. Laverne tucked it under her arm, and kept on moving—

Arkive Audio 29/a:

> *. . . We found no hog sign the second day and I lost my Kodak somewhere. Maybe I threw it away. My riding boots were chafing my heels and I was sore all over . . .*
>
> —ZNH reading *Tell My Horse* (likely to self)
> [recovered voice riff; some parts inaudible
> due to background rain]

Exposure II [Kodak Junior Six-16]

Ms. Z. under the Kindah tree at Accompong, July, 1936. And there is someone next to her—a young boy. They call him Cue Boy. He disappeared in 1804 but always comes back, on cue. The truth is, he was named Quaco, but after that it became Cuba, and after that, Cue Boy. He turns up in many photographs in Jamaica—the person you don't remember being at the family gathering. Most people don't know it, but if they look through their albums, he is there. He likes birds and trees and bodies of water, and has broad flat feet. If you look closely, you might also see that he has nine fingers. So anyway, it is mango season and there is drop-down fruit everywhere; Cue Boy is looking at the feather in Ms. Z's hat; and she has a big smile on her face because she is finally under the ancient Kindah. Ms. Z. has no idea that Cue Boy is next to her.*

They say the maroons signed their treaty with the British, under the ancient "kindah" mango tree in 1739. This was long before dutty Thistlewood, that wretched slave owner, planted mango seeds in his garden in 1773 and most definitely before official reports of the mango's first arrival. According to such reports, mango did not come to Jamaica until 1782; for the story goes that Captain Marshall's ship, Flora, (part of Lord Rodney's fleet) captured a French vessel en route from Mauritius to Haiti. There were many plants on board, including mangoes—each plant numbered, hence the famous No.11. They say the collection was delivered to one Mr. East's garden.

The half has never yet been told, but arkive it good: A mango seed. A British slaver. A Malagasy woman and her marvellous hair. Even Cue Boy knows.

Exposure III [Kodak Junior Six-16]

A nanny goat tied to a tree. Ackee? And look. There's a child peeping from behind the trunk. You can barely see her—but there is her nose; her eye and the top of her forehead. She could be about eleven, or twelve. The mass of hair on her head blends into the bark. And under the tree—what's that? Ms. Z's notebook? Held against the wind with a stone. And look, to the upper left—a black bird goes *whirr-whirr.*

of blackbird;ness [or, herstory recorded]

3likklebirds/3likklebirds/3likklebirds/

One of the few habitats of *Nesopsar nigerrimus*, the Jamaican blackbird, can be found in the Cockpit Country—that interior limestone region, responsible for the race course of history. Story has it that in the 18th century, the blackbirds saw everything, including a lost soldier who threw off his boots and red jacket; then shot himself. A runaway found the jacket, tore a piece to wrap her hair; put his boots on her feet.

Today, blackbird populations are in decline, in part because of Bauxite mining in the area.

Bauxite is the ore used to make aluminum.

Aluminum soda cans breathe under sea; they are easy to forget.

Forgetting is the condition that brings on decline of ancestor wheel-&-come.

Ornithologists describe a *Nesopsar nigerrimus*'s call as "reminiscent of the sounds of the motors of a film camera."

Oh great documentarians, were you there when—

of Ms. Z.

The children watched Ms. Z. for weeks. Wondered at her white teeth; the feather on her hat. And how she flung back her head when she laughed. The mosquitoes loved Ms. Z's brown legs. Little red bumps in constellation across her calves. And what kinda English was that she spoke? Every now and then the children made out a word, "come," "honey," or, "hallelujah." They liked "hallelujah" best. This woman knew how to say it—all music and angel's trumpet flowers-sweet.

But what was she doing here? Just hanging around. American women have time to skylark, their mothers said. They get paid to mind other people's business. Only a few months earlier, another one—Ms. Dunham—had been there. A pretty woman who liked to dance. She left with a suitcase full of fife and drum and guzu tings to take back to the States.

At night, this Ms. Z. wrote in a book. The children looked over the windowsill and saw. Sometimes she wrote letters too. Licked the envelopes three times back and forth with her tongue, then sealed them.

In the day, she sat on the colonel's verandah and waited. What for? Sometimes people took her for walks in the woodland. She was seen with Balm Woman. She liked to talk to people on the road. And she liked to eat. She love her belly, their mothers said. And how the children loved Ms. Z.—she gave them coins and mints. Only one girl, Laverne, was too shy. The American eyes were kind but too eager; and the red bumps on her legs were beginning to fester.

Laverne never found out how Ms. Zora knew that she could see soon-come things. But then again, everyone knew and came to her to read their fortune. Laverne traced their lives in the barks of trees and the veins of leaves. One day, Ms. Zora saw her on the road and stopped to talk. She picked a croton leaf* and asked Laverne to read it. Cue Boy was watching from across the way, but no one saw.

---

* *A mysterious thing is a croton leaf. Make friends with this plant and pay nuff respect. Like many travelers, it came to this island with deep secrets. The women wheeling and dancing in the spirit at the Tabernacle of Mt. Zion know this. They cut fresh leaves to adorn an altar table. No wonder Laverne saw soon-come in it. As you entah the arkive, pay attention to this and other plants along the way. And check this, be mindful of egg-shell and drop-down feathers too.*

NOTES TOWARDS ARKIVAL METHOD

Dr. Robinson's snow goose, Bower's River, Clarendon, 1758, is to date, the earliest record of a goose in Jamaica. "Bird of passage," she was.

Where did she go?

Flight feathers make the best quills, they say. On 18th century cargo lists to Jamaica there are "goose quills by the thousand." Crows will do, but geese are best for all those treaties of treaties; laws of laws; whereas of whereas—

Quill feathers make scratchy-scratchy sound on paper; history is noisy.

Listen:

If birds lose their flight feathers, they cannot fly.

Dragonfly; Erythrodiplax bromeliicola; aka, "needlecase," likes Jamaica, and Cuba too. Swarms are a rare-rare phenomenon, but with chance and patience may be glimpsed throughout the arkive, especially along its rivers. Dragonflies hold the record for longest insect migration. Swarms of thousands and even millions—once in a blue-blak—ride above water, catching frequency groove in the quantum riddim. Tip: grow indigo bromeliads in a riff of dreaming yard just before wake-up.

Monoplane: Solstice, December 21st., 1911 [Knutsford Park Race Course]

The first plane to take to the Jamaica skies is a Moisant monoplane sewn of birchwood and silk; it is a foreign insect. A crowd gathers, a thousand strong—but only those who can pay. The grandstand, of course, is best.

The wing of Air Jamaica flight 0214; Kingston, to Miami, June 29, 2015
[Aircraft Boneyard/ Tuscon, Arizona]

In this plane's better days, a young woman in seat 20A/window watched its wing. She had an iron-rust horseshoe in her bag, and wore uncomfortable shoes. She also had a copy of Ms. Z.'s *Their Eyes Were Watching.* As she looked down at the sea, her own eyes were sad like the monk seal's she thought she saw there, but which she couldn't have—because they were by then long-time extinct. True?

Snapshot I [disposable camera w/ yellow cardboard casing]

For this is her story too—this little sista from seat 20A. She was assigned seat 20D/aisle, but 20A was vacant, so she slipped over. Here she is later—in NJ—at a sewing machine. She calls herself AD. The first letter is from her great-great grandmother; the second is from the Scots who kept slaves up in the hills of Jamaica two centuries ago. By day, she works at an alteration shop in Newark, NJ. She sews in zippers and mends hems. She is undocumented; no one must know. In the arkive she is known as 20A/window.

She arrived in Newark with two books, five dresses, and a rusty horseshoe in her zip-up suitcase. The week before she left Jamaica, she was raking mango leaves in the yard when she found the horseshoe. Strange, she thought, for Kingston is not a place of many horses. She put it in the suitcase, between the book of devotions from her grandmother and the Ms. Z. novel she won for best essay at school. Ms. Z. smiled from the back cover with her jump-at-the-sun gaze. Our sista zipped the suitcase shut, and went back to raking leaves. "Wanted Dread and Alive" played on the radio.

The next week as she entered the plane, she thought she heard hooves behind her; and almost turned around to look but felt foolish doing so.

a concise history of sound

For there is a history of galloping on this island. If you listen carefully, the sound underscores everything. Hear it: dubbed in faint on a reggae track. In a hurricane. In a flock of egrets.

Colonel Rowe told Zora that in the 18th century the British soldiers and their horses were no match for the treacherous terrain of the Cockpit Country. The horses' hooves got stuck in the limestone and the runaway slaves disappeared into the hills and could not be found. He told her this, his eyes searching the bush for wild hog.

of horse run; and butterflies; and parallel dream;ing

Late one night when it is NJ snowing outside, 20A/window listens to old riddims and falls asleep on her narrow bed and dreams of the iron shoe still in her suitcase (next to the Z. book) and of the smell of mint leaves, just broken; and of a huge black and yellow-yellow butterfly with electric antennae; and of a horse named Zachariah with cocoa-tea coat and strong legs.

In 1780 Zachariah's job was to pull the wagon from Falmouth to Warren Plantation. The wagon with the new slaves in it—one of them a woman they named Abba. In the dream, Abba's eyes are stone from no more tears; but looking out on the landscape of fern and bamboo, she feels the dreamer's sleep-breath on her arm.

Dreamer-sis turns in her sleep as the wagon wheels battle the uneven road; the butterfly watches; Zachariah's cocoa-tea coat twitches.

her dream membrane [duppy wallpaper]1.*

/kozmix @ 740 hz. hello?

//nothing like a good record-scratch/needle jump/on live radio—
upnow/fi-wi

—mmm—···· onestop station/the cough/onboardtheHenriettaMarie/the-
keeper-of-lists

inthehouseofdread/ record-scratch; ing/train jump; ing, on live

radio/xeno/foreignher/tellus,   earth—tellus, is this ting real, or is it/a
cough/at fi-wi

onestop/riva-run/gully-jump/foot-stomp/hoof-flight/sea, she rising/
ooman/I-rising/time-now?

upnow, up now—mango-time/footjump/bomb bay/black-skin/No, ff FM/
one-drop

cough;ing/double-spin hustle;ing/hoof-wing ···· —eelll— dream;ing—

          sea, she-rising; up now/up,   now, butter;fly—
               and you, you run——ning in a foreign la/nd, the ancestor pant/

ing beside you, are no/less;   **hello? we're on the air.**

---

* *mem/brane: the outer veil, skin or parchment of a dream; a semi-permeable layer of
processes and synergies facilitating storage and transmission of ancestor wheel-&-come.
No fear—membranes vibrate and chant and make no sense, until they do. They are the
"frequency yard;" aka, "duppy wallpaper" of the arkive.*

i.

> *. . . she was prone to strange dreams, which came to her suddenly while*
> *working or while conversing with her fellow slaves. In one of these she*
> *saw a ship's deck with black men in murderous revolt and white men*
> *lying in crimson stains upon the flooring. In another she was on a ship*
> *at night and a negro woman, clasping a child to her bosom, crept from*
> *below and leaped into the sea. The old mammies to whom she told these*
> *dreams were wont to nod knowingly and say. "I reckon youse one o'*
> *dem Shantees, 'chile." For they knew the tradition of the unconquerable*
> *Ashantee blood, which in a slave made him a thorn in the side of the*
> *planter or cane grower whose property he became, so that few of that*
> *race were in bondage.*

"On Harriet Tubman" *San Francisco Call,*
Vol. 102, No. 121, 29th September, 1907.

ii.

Shante dreaming is a requisite* for accessing the at-risk arkive of mi-
grants and fugitives, of rebel ancestors, underground-crossings, sea-walk,
border blaze, kin shipment, and blood I-rising.

iii.

The Jamaican Swallowtail butterfly, *Papilio homerus*—the largest butterfly
in the Western Hemisphere—is the insignia of the Jamaica Kollection
of the Shante Dream Arkive. This endangered butterfly is found only in
the remote Cockpit Country and in the place where the Blue and John
Crow mountains meet, but encountered every now and
then in dreams—a wingsrush of black & yellow-yellow &
just a swish of blue—caught from a corner-eye; or on much

---

* *Kurata's note: The other requisite is imagi©nation.*

rarer occasions, landing on the dreamer's head or shoulder. The females are the largest and sail with a wingspan of up to six inches. In the 18th century the *Papilio homerus* was named after the poet, Homer, but there is reason to imagine that when Africans first saw her, they called her Shante. In the dream arkive she is called, *simply boss.*

iv.

Harriet Tubman passed over in 1913. She said, "keep running."

20A: riva run

Next morning in cold December, 20A

//wakes up with a mind to run. How curious, for she is not a runner. In the morning she likes mint tea with a quarter-teaspoon brown sugar, a little music on the radio, maybe; but not running.

But all night she has been dreaming of running along a riva she once knew. In the dream she runs and runs, pushing forward; her legs learning their power. She never knew she had legs like this. The riva urges her on, her feet familiar with every curve, every incline and dip of its path, her shoes on sure ground. The ground holds her, supports her. If she falls, it catches her. And the air, it kisses her as she runs through it. She parts it with her body—it opens for her like silence making way. There are damp leaves on the path, and rotten guava. There are three stray dogs. They chase her a piece of the way, but soon give up; barkless. For there is no sound but her. She runs so-far and so-long, that she *becomes* sound. Her feet, in nyambic beat. Sound moving through silence, drumming the red earth—

By morning when she

//awakes, the will to run is inscribed on her every cell.

THE UNMARKED GRAVE CLUB
OF WOMEN GENIUSES

As soon as Ms. Z. broke the stem, the pores on the leaf's underside gasped. Laverne saw it all—the little surface holes open wide and then close; the leaf-tip curl over like a scorpion tail. But something was not right. The green water in the veins was too still.

Laverne put the leaf back in Ms. Z's palm. *Open the gate, Ms.,* is all she said, but when Ms. pressed her further, wanting to know more, she could not say what she meant by her words.

Exposure IV [Kodak Junior Six-16]

Later, while sitting on Colonel's verandah, Ms. Z. felt someone pull at her earring—a fleeting thing—light and quick. They were drinking cerasee tea, and she found it a bitter drink. Colonel had boiled a little ganja in it too, "for the healing of cares-of-life," he said. Back in Eatonville, Ms. Z's people did not drink ganja tea, and she did not know ganja ways.* When Cue Boy flicked at her earring again, she turned around; saw Colonel Rowe standing in the doorway. Ms. Z. also did not know ancestor ways, not salt-&-sugar ancestor anyway. Colonel smiled; he liked observing this American. He picked up her camera and took a picture.

Out front, in the breadfruit tree, there was a blackbird whirring—the only reason informants know what really happened.

* *Cannabis sativa; aka: look-here; aka: duppy gyal. Some of the earliest ganja seeds were brought to this salt-&-sugar island by Indian "indentured servants." According to Shante arkival records, one man came with a few seeds hidden in the sole of his shoe; he planted them at first opportunity. When the plant grew, he named it after his mother, Lakshmi. Later, he had children with a Black woman from Lionel Town—the children called him Dada. In the years to come, subsequent descendants forgot his true name. When Ms. Z. drank ganja tea on Colonel Rowe's verandah, she did not know that she was drinking Lakshmi—Lakshmi who died waiting for her one-son to send a letter.*

Years before her trip to Jamaica, Ms. Z collected folklore in Polk County, Florida. She arrived with a car and nice Harlem clothes. Too many bells, she soon realised. No one trusted her; they would not share their stories. *Is she a spy?* folk must have wondered. *A police detective?*

That's when she changed her identity, made herself out to be a bootlegger—a fugitive on the run. This new story accounted for her car, fancy clothes and up-north talk. Ah, the people thought now. She's one of us.

In Jamaica, drinking ganja tea (spiked with a touch of rum) on an Accompong verandah, and slapping mosquitoes around her ankles, she told the same story—this time, former bootlegger turned Guggenheim scholar. We know this, from the big smile on the colonel's face in *Exposure V*, a bottle of white rum on the table. His glass half full, Ms. Z's empty.

And too, she also told the truth.

"My father was the mayor of Eatonville, FL," she said, "a town founded by ex-slaves and their descendants, the first all-black community in the States."

Colonel Rowe listened, feeling something kindred with John Hurston and his fire-boned daughter. And he told her the story of the Accompong people, how they ran with their feet in their hands and founded this steal-away community. How the British soldiers and their too-red jackets were no match for the Cockpit Country; no match for the art of camouflage. How because of that, the maroons were self-ruled since 1739.

That night, though, the Colonel did not tell the magic things—raw moon and black wiss and guzum strength. But he read the freckles on Ms. Z's cheekbone, and knew that was what she really craved.

They say Ms. Z. left on a van to Kingston in September. She was wearing a navy blue dress and a sideways hat on her head. Laverne Downs stood at the roadside, watching. Ms. Z. turned and their eyes met; silent words—*open the gate*—passing between them. Ms. Z smiled and blew her a kiss. Cue Boy watched from under a guango tree.

Ms. Z's was a curious life to read, Laverne saw. There were no children in view. But there were words. So many of them. She saw black ink on wide sheets on a clothesline; the wind blowing the sheets like God's sermon. God's eyes are watching her, she thought.

A week later in Haiti, Zora sat at a table in a house with rain falling-falling on the zinc roof. She wrote her novel with the rain pouring down, beating the windows. The words came rushing out-all—in seven weeks—and only then did she understand the girl Laverne's words. That story was "dammed up in me."

Back home in New York, she sent Laverne thanks, and a present—a box of tarot cards; the *Rider-Waite,* recently designed by a Ms. Pamela Coleman Smith.* "You have divine sight," she wrote.

---

* Ms. Coleman Smith—a high priestess of the Unmarked Grave Club of Woman Geniuses, ate Kingston mango as a girl; listened Anancy story; went off to England, designed
her 78 cards. According to herstorical and kuratorial accounts, she passed Zora in the
middle of the street in Harlem once. It was summer and breezy, and the hems of their
skirts touched.
  Note: high priestesses of UGCWG appear throughout the arkive.

through the open gate: 20A/window, dream-chant;ing
[after chloe wofford]

Ms. Z's words run on the page; god's eyes are watching as they run; Janie and Tea Cake run run run; run Janie; run, on the page; the page is a good place for running; if you run on the page no one can catch you; not massa; not god; not flood water; not Homeland Security; run Zora, run; run on the page; this is how you write a book in seven weeks—

BE/WARE: ENDANGERED ARKIVE

[cough]; also, ewa; also, ikó; also, ụkwarà; also, kosuk; also, ketiketoo; also—

The bell of the Henrietta Marie *was found in 1972 and is the property of a Florida museum; the cough, on the other hand, exists only in the Shante Arkive. As you feel into the sound, you might experience a scratchiness in your throat; don't be alarmed. It belonged to a woman in the hull of the ship who coughed each time she heard the bell. The bell rang every thirty minutes—a haunting, foggy D5 sound. The captain kept time, but the woman kept memory. Each time the bell rang, she coughed to remember herself. She was squeezed tight between two others—one of them pregnant-and-vomit; the other, a girl-chile who cried.*

freedom paper, 1773; [item 110]

This "free-paper" was found between the pages of a King James Bible—in the Book of Isaiah to be precise. The Bible itself is also of interest. It was discovered in an iron trunk under an old house in Clarendon. How many years had it been there? The Bible is watermarked and worn, but the freedom paper is relatively undamaged.

They say the slave girl—Tomer—from Warren Plantation, was fifteen years old at the writing of this document. This paper declares her free in another fifteen. John Warren wrote the document on his deathbed because he knew the girl to be his daughter and because each time she looked at him, he saw his mother in her wandering left eye. The eye wandered ever so slightly to the left, but enough to prick him.

The story behind this artifakt is that Tomer died in childbirth on July 11, 1788, the same-same day she was to turn free. She never got to sing freedom song. At the time of her death, the free-paper was hidden in her hair, tucked deep into her plaits, having been given to her that very morning by Warren's son come-from-England.

They called the slave woman, Abba, to prepare the body for burial—Abba who knew how to wash and mend Mistress's silk things, and skin and carve a cow too. Abba bathed Tomer in bayleaf water, cleaned her navel and the grit between her toes; rubbed her down with coconut oil. She undid scarf and plaits, the hair dusty with cane blossom, and that's when she found it—the freedom paper—hidden there in the deep. Outside, Tomer's new-born cried with the July crickets.

It was tea time, the Great House all ginger cake and china plate. Abba took the free-paper and pushed it in her bosom. That night, she ran.

2oA remembers* hearing this story: A woman goes to America, an "illegal alien," and receives a social security number—a false one. The SS# is given to her by a relative. "Use this," he says, and his eyes add, "Don't ask any more questions." She takes it because she is eighteen, and afraid—of her relative, and of America, and of the INS, and because the Caribbean Sea is too wide and treacherous and she cannot turn back now. And she takes it because of shame. If she does not survive in America, she will return home in shame.

Many years later, after she has forsaken the false number and become a U.S. citizen, she wonders: Where did he get the number? Did he make it up? Did he find it in the trash? Did it belong to a dead person? She imagines a man—dead. How did he die?

She does not regret taking the number. From way-way on the other side, the dead man sees her write it—next to her name; and he feels the same sort of pleasure the dead feel after donating a pair of good eyes, a liver, or a clean heart.

and so it is,

Abba takes the free paper and runs. She runs through macca and limestone, over hill and gully. She runs. She has heard of a place, a far away place. Her feet will lead her to where it is.

At daybreak, she comes across a wild sow and her four piglets in the bush. The mother sees her and snorts with such force that black birds in the tree above, scatter. Not even Mistress's hounds are a match for a wild sow. But Abba, for reasons she does not know herself, begins to hum. She stands there, rooted in her spot and hums. The song takes her across sea,

---

* *Kurata's Note: A third requisite for access to the arkive is memory. Do we trust it?*

to far-home Africa; and to her mother grinding millet in a clearing. And to the sun on the back of her neck; the sound of the pestle in the mortar; her mother's voice, yellow millet strong.

A black and yellow-yellow butterfly the breadth of one of Mistress's cake plates pitches on a leaf. The wild sow puffs a half-puff, then lies down; her piglets suck at her teats. Abba hums; the sow's ear twitches; the butterfly waits—

her bootleg; or, the art of camouflage II 👁 ᐟᐟ

According to studies, butterflies can see patterns—not visible to humans—on each other's wings.

Caribbean squid and octopus deep in the blue-blue, play mas—camouflaging as redrock and seaweed and coral-gal.

In the Cockpit Country, fugitive slaves secreted themselves in limestone caves that dipped and turned and covered their tracks and their backs. The Red-coats circled in the tropic heat.

Our great-and-grand mothers flour-pasted their walls with "pretty-paper" from magazines, newspapers, biscuit wrap, and old calendars. It made the wattle wall nice but evil spirits who came to the door, were fatigued by the pitchy-patchy, and walked away.

This open secret: in Jamaica we fear those big, dark moths that fly into our homes at night and rest above a picture frame, or a mirror, or a favourite plant; they stay there for hours and hours while we cuss and pray. Fear not, for they pitch and watch, mesmerized only by our true patterns—the ones not even we can see.

on sleep walk;ing

The girl, Laverne, walks in her sleep. She climbs out of bed and opens the front door, stands in the yard and listens to the sky. Across sea, Ms. Z. click-clicks at the alphabet. And somewhere, oars lap against water.

But if Laverne holds still, just-so, she can hear the echo of three hundred years. A goat-skin drum. And under that, feet running through bramble. And deeper still, mortar and pestle.

And if she bends on her knees; puts her ear to the ground, just-so, she can hear train-rush—iron/clash/tin/steel away/underground/ tin/pan from the future/*next stop*/ iron/clash/tin/steel away/*next stop, Penn Station.*

The stars over Accompong hum softly; they are too stubborn to fall.

oh-night

Are there stars over Newark?

HOW RUNNERS ARE BRED

For here is 20A's story—

In her story, the ICE officers come to the alteration shop while she is stitching hems. They come with their cross-questions and notebooks. They ask for her passport; her green card. I left it at home, she says. They search her purse. (Do they have the right?) They unfold the receipts. They find the one photo she has of Gramma. O Grams; sweet Grams, standing in the doorway with her cane. Who is this woman? they ask. And who is this boy? That's when she notices him for the first time—a small boy off to the side, watching; only one foot in the frame. They ask who owns this shop; does she use street drugs; is there a boyfriend; they give her twenty-four hours to report to the agency, then turn to leave. "Bloodfiah," she says, and her voice surprises her; so strong and out-loud. The two officers pause, then walk through the door letting it slam behind them; their shoes leave mud on the shop floor.

How she wish-wishes she had a dead man's SS number.

In this part of town, if you run, people assume you are fleeing trouble. Today, she has half the money meant for her late rent; she grabs her bag, and heads for the street—any street—to take her out of Newark. Run, girl! a boy calls. She feels self-conscious, but keeps going; no river in this place, but there's a concrete trench filled with soda cans, cigarette butts and beer bottles; she crosses a bridge; sprints past an elementary school and auto repair; freezing rain settles on her cheekbones; it is getting late; she doesn't know where to turn.

But, this is what she remembers in her flight: the betting shop not far from the Kingston house she grew up in. Tosh on speakers across the way. The men-there rooting for No. 11, Miracle Girl.

of running & horses & ships at the horizon

Yes true, there is a history of running on this island. It began with the Taino running into the hills upon seeing three ships on the horizon. And then there were the horses. The first horse was introduced in 1509. By the mid-sixteen hundreds, they were wild and running everywhere. "The very vermin of the country," someone said. Then there were the African slaves. And the dogs to chase them. Every track and field champion inhabits this history. And so does the woman running for her bus, and the man fleeing gunshot. And our 20A running across a four-way intersection.

—a small cry from inside the cloth at her back,

pauses Abba mid-note. It is the baby—Tomer's new-born. Abba hadn't the heart to leave without him—a boy baby—his palms criss-crossed with signs and wonders. It was easy to fall in love. To muffle his cry, she bound up his mouth gentle as she could, wrapped him in a blanket and tied him to her back. Deep in the hills now, she quickly gives him her dry breast. But it has been a long night and she is beginning to doubt the wisdom of it all. He cries and cries, and is so tiny, and weak.

But she sees now, the sow is injured. A hind leg broken—perhaps while escaping from hunters—and the animal has lost most of its strength. Standing in the clearing, Abba knows what she must do. She breathes in from her belly-bottom and keeps humming her mother's millet song. The sow closes its eyes and Abba inches a little closer. The four piglets suckle as if there is no tomorrow. The closer Abba edges, the deeper she hums. She puts the baby boy at the sow's teats, and he sucks wild milk. The cake-plate butterfly, still pitched on the leaf, opens and closes its wings; slow-slow now, slow-slow.

For just one moment, Abba thinks about leaving the baby there to rest with the hog and its four piglets. She could go quick-search for seed or nut; leftover rainwata. But the little boy opens one eye and looks at her as if to warn, *don't*. So she sits and leans against the tree and hums and hums and thinks of her mother's millet cakes and almost wishes for a hog's teat.

Morning, baby-boy tied to her back, she finds overripe soursop and fallen naseberry in the bush. And trudges on, chased by wasps and rain and a flight of black birds. She is wearing Tomer's shoes—old hand-me-downs from mistress's daughter. The fronts are cut off, so there is more space for toes; her skirt is hitched up so it comes to her knee. Miles and miles of poisonwood and mahoe lay ahead.

She has heard of a place. A far-off place—

signs & wonders

They say even two hundred years later, Cue Boy roams this island because he was nursed by a wild hog's teat. They say if he stands next to you under a mango tree, you will lose something but it will turn up again in an unusual way. Maybe that's why so many of us have feelings of wheel-&-come. They say he means well, but can't help it. If he visits your yard, it will grow unusually beautiful. He will attract birds, and if there are pea doves, they will chant-it-again, but brand new. Your dreams will be filled with horses. Your clock will stop ticking. He will leave you feather gifts. And for no particular reason, you might feel the urge to run.

swing low

By the time the deck of cards arrived at Accompong, the package was torn and falling apart. The children gathered around to see what was inside. No one knew what to make of the cards. Someone said, Obeah, they look like obeah. That's when Laverne's mother hid them under the mattress. Touch them and I beat you, she said.

Later, the cards blew away in the 1944 hurricane. This was before hurricanes were christened, but sure enough, the next storm after that got a name—Charlie. In 1944 the cards whirled hurry-wind to the far reaches of the island, bringing divination to the people. A Lovers card got caught between the slats of someone's window; a Four of Wands flew with such speed, it slashed a woman's eye; and the Chariot, well, it got lodged under the minute hand of the clock tower at Half Way Tree.

In 1937 when Laverne opened the package and saw the Chariot card, she heard horses, and then, a cacophony of backed up traffic, car horns and buses coming from the future. She also heard running feet.

All 78 cards still exist. They are tucked into books, Bibles, floorboards and drawers. One is buried with a corpse in May Pen Cemetery. Many have rotted in soil, and plants grow in their place. They exist as cerasee and ramgoat dashalong and leaf of life and mango and guava and lignum vitae. There is one card which remains in the turret of St. Andrew Parish Church—the Hermit. The Chariot card fell from behind the clock's minute hand, but was found years later by a woman crossing a street. She heard horse-neigh coming from her headphones, tucked the card in her bag and ran to catch the downtown bus.

horse latitudes

The horses came on ships; they crossed the Atlantic with the Spanish Conquistadors. They were kept below, strapped with slings around their chest and belly, suspended to rafters so only hind feet touched the ground. In the dark of the ship's belly, they slept with eyes open and dreamed of galloping on roaring water. Some survived shipwreck; found this island and swam ashore. Others drowned, their knees weak from dreaming. There were voyages on which, for lack of water, some were thrown overboard—victims of that slow-riddim calm between 30 degrees north and 30 degrees south of the shequator where tropic breeze, caught in a groove, refuses to blow, and ships cannot sail.

The creoles—bred in Kingston pens, one-room tenement yards—wondered at the sea-rockaway memories that made their coats twitch. Those that came via Cuba had glimpsed our horizon from the harbour at Havana. A few became plantation aristocrats—slaves fanning flies away from their rear as they switched their tails. But most were taken to the mainland; little did they know that they would become the story of the American West.

In a study of long-time memory it was found that horses have recall like a DJ rewind; and in the 18th century, some, remembering the hull and howl of Africans on the Atlantic,

could not be tamed.

[cough]; also, ewa; also, ikó; also, u̱kwarà; also, kosuk; also, ketiketoo; also—

In the journey from Calabar to Port Royal, the bell of the Henrietta Marie *rang approximately 3,840 times; and Ashante woman coughed 3,206 times, each a remembrance. A small cough to remember self and name—Adwoa. Or, to remember her mother's name. Or, her mother's mother's name. To remember. The forest she loved to walked in. And a certain tree in the forest. And a certain fruit on the tree. And a certain seed in the fruit. To remember. The river she washed herself in. And certain fish in the river. And certain bones in the fish. To remember. The sky and certain stars in the sky. And a certain hum in the stars.*

The 3,206 coughs have been retrieved—sieved from wail-and-bawl, passage cuss, ship phlegm, whip-shout, sea wheeze, horse neigh and baby cry.

run natty run

Evening, and 20A is tired. She sits on the edge of a bench; dandelions grow in the cracks around it. She takes the horseshoe from the bag and fits it against her heel—the iron, strangely warm. When she leans into the bench, the shoe falls to the ground. Sleep comes quickly—

In her dream she arrives, again, at Warren Plantation, the horse, Zachariah, flicks flies with its tail; wonders at the sound of far-away feet. She unhitches his rope from the fence, sets him free and he gallops across loot-and-fiah. Already miles into the hills, she sees Abba moving between trees. Abba pauses—quick—to grab fall-down rose apple; 20A takes one too and bites it; Abba thinks the warm breath at her shoulder is an ancestor come to greet her—not a dreamer. 20A tries to speak, but no sound comes. She wants to whisper, *keep going,* but the words won't come. The baby makes a muffled cry. *I hear him,* she wants to say. She kisses his forehead with her sleep lips instead; it calms him—just a bit. Abba sneezes as piss-a-bed puffs little parachutes—

20A //wakes before a man reaches for her horseshoe. She grabs it quick, and puts it back in the bag. There is a Greyhound bus station not far away. She will use the rent money and buy a ticket to Arizona. She has heard that the Grand Canyon is America at its most open-hearted; that it is wide enough and big enough to hold everything. She will go there, and shout her name.

the kuration of dreams

For the dreamers clear our footpaths. They run behind and before, find traps up ahead, sweep broken glass, divert the gaze of enemies. The dreamers step in the paths of gunshot, take the stone in the eye, open the door so we'll slip through. They breathe against our ear when we are lonely. Laugh when no one else gets the joke.

Who from the future is dreaming you?

And from the past, who dreams you?

The artifakt of present time is a collaboration, a meeting of dreams.

The long-time dead and the yet-to-come have dreamed us here. And we have dreamed them.

Who is dreaming you now, clearing the obstacles in your path?

jah chariot

And rainy season came and went, and flood waters receded, and Bombays blossomed and mangoes fell, and the black birds went whirr-whirr—

And Laverne sat in the yard burning from the beating for taking the Chariot from under the mattress, when she saw the future floating toward her on a dandelion parachute. A seed was still stuck to the bottom of the stem, and it landed on her knee, so soft she almost missed the story held inside* and the word which came to her: *run.*

This is how she left Accompong.

* Cassia occidentalis, *Jamaican dandelion; or, piss-a-bed*

Dandelions were brought to the Americas with intention, and now, they are destroyed with intention. Yellow-yellow rebel gyal, how angry people are at your thriving.

Exposure VI [Kodak Junior Six-16]

A man with a wild hog. Colonel Rowe? He has slit the throat and there is blood on his shirt. In the end, it took three days, three dogs and three men to corner the hog. Ms. Z climbed onto a rock and watched the final showdown. So did Cue Boy. See the boy in the corner with his hands covering his eyes?

Later, Z. tells Colonel the story told to her of how she learned how to walk. She was still a crawling baby when her mother left her briefly to run out into the yard. Little Ms. Z. was sitting on the floor eating a piece of cornbread when in came a sow and her piglets through the open door. Her mother heard her cry and came rushing back—there was little Ms. Z.—holding on to the bed and standing up, all by herself, for the first time.

This is how she made her first steps.

And this is how she made it to Harlem, a jump-at-the-sun look in her eye.

And this is how she wrote *Their Eyes*.

And this is how when our sista in seat 20A won it for best essay, she felt the world was big enough to hold her. And why should she let that feeling go now?

1/*wheelin, wheelin*

Someone said matter can neither be created nor destroyed. Is this true? If so, then there is material evidence everywhere.

Memories, on the other hand, can be both created and destroyed. If this is true, then we are all mothers and fathers of invention.

Dreams reside in the spaces between memory and matter. This is why in lucid dreams the words of a book are interchangeable. When dreaming it is best to read while running. In this way, you will remember deeply. And when reading it is best to run while dreaming. Run run run through the open gate! This way, you will recognize evidence when you find it.

For they say, like dreams, our stories dwell in that liminal space—we live and breathe and cheer each other on there.

As somewhere in a Kingston betting shop, a horse leaps across the finish line &—

[APERTURE; OR, UN/COMMON PASSAGE]

oh?

—the world record for a horse's long jump is 27 ft. 6 in. At this writing, for humans it is 29 ft. 4 1/4 in. The truth is though, there are greater feats which have gone unrecorded.

During Hurricane Gilbert, a mother is said to have jumped a horizontal distance of 33 ft. 4 in. to save the baby whipped out of her arms by the wind. True, her leap was aided by hurricane force, but one cannot disregard the power of love—so precise—that she caught the baby, mid-air, seconds before a sheet of zinc would have sliced its neck.

& then there is the story of how the runaway, Abba—when she heard overseer behind her—leaped with Baby Quaco, across limestone rock. No statistical records, but it was a leap of unparalleled danger, for not even the overseer with his long legs and big boots could traverse such a pit.

She landed on her two feet, her hand-me-down shoes ripped heel to toe, Quaco stunned to silence. This was only the beginning.

For such a leap opens fissures which last for centuries. To this day, it is said that if you go to that place, there is a cleft in the air. Stretch your arm &—you feel it—the air move like the parting of the Red Sea.

so shush;

& arrive—here; between words on a page; between the oscillations of guitar strings; at the boiling point of ginger tea; the high arc of a child's swing

ing—just-so/just-so;

a weary woman found such a place in the crack of a plate—

it was the humming from inside the porcelain which made her first notice. A far-away alto; timbre of wood smoke & cocoa pod—

The plate fell from her hands, broke in two; she picked up the pieces & there it was—a landscape-opened-up; a path & a dim light—

& she walked right through it.

An old man with a bag of guavas was there to meet her. Other people have come this way before, he said. Don't mind your step. Mud on the feet is a baptism.

& too, there is the young man at the Half Way Tree crosswalk; a sensation of C sharp at the base of his spine. He paused; sound travelling him far back—for one flicker—a glimpse of—a boy hanging from a tree?

but, the light is about to change now, & there is a bus to catch—

Such apertures open up when we—

leap like outlaws,

unlatch the ampersand of the dream—

THE FACE YOU DON'T SEE
UNTIL YOU DEVELOP THE NEGATIVE

and blinked. To adjust to sudden cold. And. A curious half light. The sky all silver-grey fish scales. She crouched in. A stand of; crooked no-leaf trees. And; over there

a girl with three-plaits-&-lace-boots throwing feed. To long-necked birds. The girl spoke quiet-quiet, half to Abba and, half to herself—*He fattens his geese and plucks they feathers for his quill pens.*

Afterwards, they hold they necks high, but cannot fly. I feeds them corn. What plantation you run from?

—What them call here?

—*Cello.*

—Why it so cold?

—*Shhh . . .*

Quaco, who had been quiet, made a little moaning sound then. Abba reached into the cloth tied to her back to take him out and offer a dry tit. The warmth of his body caressed her back, but when she reached,

he was not there. She smelled baby skin,

but he was not there.

He moaned again, a small sound like a chi chi bud,

but the cloth was empty; and

he was not there.

She looked behind her; patted the ground; searched the sky,

but he was not there.

Have mercy, Lord,

the *Shhh* girl said to no one in particular—

or; the true story of how a jamaican slave came to america; virginia, 1788

They hid Abba and the babysound in a hole under the floor of a cabin. *Because what to do with this funny-talking woman who say she come from a sugar isle? And Lord, what to do with a babysound too? Chile cry like he suckle a haint's teat.*

Under the board floor it was damp and cold. Abba held her breath. Someone reached and dropped a sweet-tit into Baby Quaco's cry. Voices outside. *Yes, missus. No, missus.* A musty smell; in the distance, horses' hooves. And what kind of wind was this? It whistled and moaned a no-word language; only crosses and pain-o-heart in it; the kind that have no beginning and no end. Abba and the wind communed together. It moaned and she moaned back. It whimpered and she did too, in the same-same voice. Because trials and tribulation know each other and break tears together. And this is how woman and wind and babysound rode out the first night, Abba whimpering and Quacosound suckling.

Oi, windmodda.

Oi, night.

Oi, wheelin tings.

Oi, jesusfiah.

Oi-oi, bloodtit, fool-fool, duttysinting gal-mi.

Oi, Tomer.

She had not meant to leap so far—

of mango-time

I-niversal Truth: Light travels a distance of 5,878,625,373,184 miles in one year. No one is older than light or has travelled further. They say we live in an expanding universe, but the ancestor knew that long before Babylon. Galaxies wheel out, into I-finity.

And check this: Abba's leap and the hurricane babymother's were synsistafied; both happening at the same-same—

By next morning, baby Quaco was quiet, but had not reappeared.

waxing gibbous & undreaming before bed on a bench; (see also, *waning gibbous & redreaming after bed on a bus*)

20A found him unconscious on a rock in her dream, a sweet tit still in his mouth; a horseshoe around his little ankle; his breath a closing & opening night blooming ting; dog bark in the distance, three times; a door slam shut;

the dream replayed over and over—

a horseshoe around his little ankle; a closing & opening night blooming ting; dog bark in the distance, three times three; a moon breathing door

closing & opening night blooming distance; three barks & three doors;

the rotation too quick for her to entah—

cello

The *Shhh* girl's long-neck birds are making noise outside. Somewhere a horse neighs, but no baby cry. Abba lifts the floorboards and peeps. The room is empty; everyone left for the fields. A wood stove. A black pot hanging from a nail. Two potatoes and a pile of rags. A tin cup. Horse hooves and a massa-voice fading in the distance, but no baby cry. Through the window and across the way, the *Shhh* girl is there again; feeding the long-necks. She throws seed from a bucket and the long-necks surround her shoes-feet, the ends of her headscarf caught in wind. Something white and whiff fills the air, falls down from the sky, disappears when it touches the ground; quiet and half-remembranced and fading quick like wake time did-I-dream-it. Another horse sounds itself but still, no baby cry.

If Abba can reach *Shhh* girl without being seen, she can ask. Outside, the trees make long marks on the ground. The shadows slant sideways, pointing which way. Abba creeps, tree to tree. For the trees are kin; they hide secrets. The birds do too, and so do the ants and mites and burrowing tings. When Abba holds still, the branches steady her in a slow embrace, and when she moves, her darkness and their darkness enfold in the shadows. Across the way, the people swing hoes in a field. *Shhh* girl empties the last of her bucket, shifts the handle to the crook of a slender corn-yellow arm and walks away in muddy shoes-feet. The shoe leather is old and the laces jute twine, but they are shoes.

abba; *shoes fall* [arkive audio transcript/1]

she must have a rich massa to have shoes like that. i see him on his horse & with his jacket-tails & top hat on. fi mi neva give me none. had to take Tomer's dead-lef ones—them so small, i cut the toe-front to fit mi foot. and look how bad-lucky me is—lost them & mi baby in one leap. & mi free-paper too. in a moment, in a twinkling of an eye. you know that way? that place? is a deepness place.
    close-close & far-far

tween rockstone & years & moonshining tings
tween stars & dream & lizard croak call
& tween chichibud song & clip-clop clip-clop
tween look-here & look-behind
& the one-one hairs on yu head &
see here, tween balm leaf tings
& last abeng bawl
& breath & salt &
eyewata love & oi,
pain a yu heart

shhh

"Inside the big house, they play a game of goose. Heard it from his little miss," *Shhh* girl says soft to the rake.

"Mi baby?"

"Shhh."

"Me looking mi baby."

"Shhh."

Abba huddles under a bush; the leaves are needles that prick. The girl rakes dirt and talks to the geese, nonsense talk; she tosses left-over grain from inside a skirt pocket.

"Come, Night," she soothes in her sof-sof way, and one of them shuffles towards her. "Come, Star," she says. "Quick, Two Feets, come." The geese peck-peck; then she shoos them away.

There's a muffled cough; someone's warm breath. Abba turns, but no one is there. Geese scatter.

"Careful, hear?" *Shhh* girl says to the air.

of geese & gandering: pressure drop [unmastered]

Come dark, Abba searches for the passageway from which she had come—that patch of trees near the long-neck birds. When the big house goes to sleep, she gathers speed and runs and leaps, runs and leaps. The ground is muddy and cold; her skirt gets wet; and without shoes, her feet bleed on the stones. Hands reaching into air, she grasps for anything—grassquit/ ground lizard/ tamarind pod/jack-ass rope. But why bother? On the other side of the leap the Jamaica hounds still bark and the night sky is as watching and as far away.

Early morning, *Shhh* girl finds Abba huddled with the chickens—quicktime covers her with sticks and dry leaves; fowl poop, feather and broken eggshell in the mix. Abba listens: *Shhh* girl with her broom and shoes-feet brushing the ground. Outside, there are voices: two massa man's—must be—for they are the only ones who talk like their mouths full of flour. The massas get closer and *Shhh* girl sweeps quicker; feathers flying; hens cluck-clucking; dust filling Abba's nose and mouth—she holds in a sneeze and pees instead. The pee runs slant across the dirt floor; stops right at the edge of the fence, almost touches the heel of massa's boot.

"Give a peck of flour to each."

"Yes, sir."

"And salted fish will do; cheaper than pork."

"Of course."

Shhh girl keeps on sweeping, the laces of her shoes-feet undone and trailing in the dust. The broom hits a basket and an egg falls to the ground. *Shhh* girl pulls in a breath, swift-swift gathers yellow yolk and shell in the hem of her skirt. The massa boots leave; there is horse clip-clop in the distance.

"Overseer not allowed his own goose, but he can whip us," *Shhh* girl says to the air.

She sweeps more dust and chicken fluff then taps the broom three times against the wall; leans it in a corner.

"Black Feets," she coos, sof-sof to a goose at the door.

"Come, Night," she soothes and one of them wanders against her calf. "Come, Star," she calls, scattering a galaxy of feed. "Quick, Two Feets, run."

she got shoes/[item 380]

Here are Abba's American shoes. This item was given to her by *Shhh* girl.
Note: one foot is larger than the other—it's the best *Shhh* girl could do.
They are once again, dead-lef shoes; deceased unknown. Wooden sole;
leather upper from an old sow died in labor. These shoes have no left or
right.

FOUND SOUND

In Newark, 20A lives in a one-room. The residence is owned by an old couple and their parrot. The whole place smells like pee; even her room. No matter how she tries, she cannot get the smell out. There is one other tenant—a young woman, Meryl. She looks at the floor when she and 20A cross paths, and rarely speaks. Sometimes she has scratches on her face and arms; one time she had a busted mouth; but her auburn hair is cut short and nice, and when she wears makeup, she looks pretty. American girl like her—20A wonders how she ended up in a place like this. 20A does make friends with the couple's parrot though. It sits in a cage by the back door and says, "Shit," when she comes in. "Yu raas," 20A replies; so now it knows how to say that too. She has two months left on the lease. The landlords do not know that ICE is after her. As long as she pays the rent, they treat her well enough; but if the government came they would turn her in quicker than the parrot could say, "Raas."

She has already spent the whole night on a bench in the Greyhound station and probably cannot get away with staying there any longer. She thinks of her narrow bed. And of the back door-slam. And the heater turned down too low. And the smell of pee in the closet. *Shit.* But even if she wanted to go back, she cannot now.

She looks at the bus schedule. After Flagstaff, the 6:50 continues to Phoenix. She only has money for as far as Flagstaff but likes this name, "Phoenix," and that the bus continues there. It leaves in ten minutes and she will need to hurry. Passengers are already at the gate; there are two men with neck-ties getting on. One of them scans the waiting room and scratches his chin. They both have big black shoes. Each time she sees a white man with a neck-tie, she worries that he could be from the government. What if one of the neck-ties got on the bus and searched it? When people are undocumented, they have such thoughts; and 20A is no different. She is always looking over her shoulder. She must make herself small. Only a short time in the U.S. and she has almost lost her accent. It happened unconsciously. Better if people don't notice you. And here now, in the Greyhound station at Newark, she does not like the look of these two neck-ties.

This is how 20A decides to wait on the next bus—in seven hours. She pays for her ticket and has $12.51 left, then goes to the restroom and waits for the 6:50 to leave. She washes her face again, and wipes under her arms with damp paper towels. Afterwards, she stands by the glass door and watches a little sparrow peck at left-over potato chips. She wishes she were a raas sparrow.

 When the AZ bus arrives, 20A looks around, sizing up the passengers—a drunk swaying from side to side; a couple of European tourists with backpacks; a guitar guy; a mother and two kids; an Amish family; and an elderly woman who talks to herself. That's when she notices the greyhound—captured mid-motion—there on the side of the bus. The hound's legs span the coach in a leap of speed and power. She knows about greyhounds. She has heard their barking in her dreams. Their noses sniffing the ground, they pant behind us as we run. The greyhounds stop at nothing. Even centuries later they can remember a scent—

come here, jesus: carmine velvet remix [found sparrow voice; audio 47/a]

The forest is all damp and dry-leaf. Night comes down and Abba walks careful-careful, not wanting to make noise—she has left her hiding place at Cello and is deep in woods. She pauses from time to time, to touch the trees; wonders at their nakedness. Something breathes inside their bark. When she leans against a granmodda-one, it hums into her back; livity rising up. The trees, them guide this way; and balm this way; and hush this way; and hush this way.

A small clearing is up ahead. The moon-clouds play shadows, but way passed the twigs and dry-up leaves, is a red singing ting.

Someone there.

A missus girlwoman sitting under a tree, picking bramble from her mess of red hair.

Missusgirl sings soft and sweet—all soprano cricket and chirp and moonbeam; she picks and sways and sings and talks to the chickadees. Abba watches from behind her tree, breathing quiet. This missusgirl full of lady button song, her voice so lullaby it makes Abba's eyes heavy. When Abba shifts her weight from one leg to the other, missgirl quick-time turns around. Lookhere: she has two centuries-old eyes, a grey cliff-jump colour with something buzzing inside. Abba steps out from behind the tree. The earth tilts a little, and the missus girlgal speaks first—

"They don't believe I'm a get it, but I am."

"Get what?"

"The world just born. Clean and new and smooth."

"Oh?"

Missusgirl breaks into a smile then. Her teeth mossy-yellow like buttercup pollen. "Ain't you a funny looking thing. You sad and ugly ones keepa comin, you do. Lost count now. Guess I been here so long—a hundred years or more, feels like. Didn't know this-here forest would be so big and so forever. More forever than the sky, it is." And she stops and looks up. "How far up them stars go you think?" She stretches her arms—wide as they can go—her shawl two tired wings. "Come here, Jesus. More forever than them stars, this forest is, more forever than even the friggin stars."

Up ahead, a chickadee whistles a four-note call. "Me looking mi baby," Abba says.

Missusgirl throws back her head and lets out a long-long laugh at that. Her mouth opens to the trees, and the laugh moves the air, gnats and midges shaken up on her shawl. She doubles over and hugs her knees and laughs some more; when she looks up, her face is pink like frangipani blossom. But this missus girlgal don't know frangipani. Abba wishes she could show her frangipani, so she could see her face. There is a place where the missus womans like her wear frangipani flowers in their broad brim hats and eat rum cake all day and sit under shady silk cotton trees—

The missusgirl has not seen Quaco; but then again, she has seen too many Quacos and too many lost moons to count. After a fit of belly laugh, she gathers her rags and leaves, singing. She heads upstream for a piece of the world just born, her voice filling the forest. Missusgirl's soprano is what sparrow whistles are made of and hurry-talking winter wind. It lingers in fly-and-gone nests in the treetops, catches in the wings of late migrating warblers. Just when Abba thinks missusgirl's voice is done, there is a yell: *They don't believe I'm a get it, but I am!* The sound echoes and the last of the leaves on a granauntie tree dislodge and fall. Abba itches to call back, to test her voice too, see how far it travels in the no-leaves. She throws a dry pine up to the sky instead.

···· ~eeeeee~ *they don't believe i'm a get it, but i am/ they don't believe i'm a get it, but i am/ they don't believe i'm a get it, but i am/* Union Station one-stop—

abba; *hear him?* [audio transcript/2]

some a them hear roof wata drippin in their head; some a them hear church bell ringin; some a them hear hissin grass-snake & speakins in modda tongue; or, a mighty roar of a mighty riva in a mighty gorge.

me? me hear baby cry.
always, Quaco cryin, cryin.

Quaco-cry come back,
but still no Quaco.

hear him?

There is a baby crying in the back of the bus. The mother stands and walks up and down the aisle trying to hush him. The baby unhinges his mouth and gives the bawl all he's got. In her distress, the mother pats his back, perhaps a tad hard. The child begins to cough. The driver comes on the speaker. *All passengers must stay seated. Please remain seated while the bus is in motion.* There is a whiff of baby puke as mother and baby walk back down the aisle. 20A shuffles in her seat. She has a headache from not enough to eat. She puts her backpack against the window and leans her head on it. When she was little, Gramma would give her warm milk sprinkled with nutmeg. Nutmeg cure plenty tings, Gramma would say. In the absence of Gramma cure, 20A imagines a nut-milk taste in her mouth. There is a prickling sensation under her tongue. Belief cure and belief kill, Gramma would say.

dreamiversal dub or; waning gibbous & redreaming after bed on a bus

When the sista from seat 20A dreams, no one asks for her green card, and the keeper of the dreamgate always lets her in. He has three tall locs that grow up to the sky, far-far into I-finity.

20A holds her head way back, but cannot see the top of them. His locs disappear into the swirling dreamity.

"Welcome, dawta," the locsman says, "the dream expands the way the I-niverse expands, for to overstand dreams is to highastand the I-niverse—know its structure and unstructure; I-finity and riddim; ways and unways."

20A looks up at the fullness of dread, puts her hand on the locman's chest to feel if he is real. His I&I beat is one she knows. When he calls her name, the sound bends space and she dips and wheels into the dream-mi-verse; all nightness magenta and free.

Asleep on the bus, 20A re-dreams the baby dream, the scene rewinding. "Uprise," says the locsman.

And this time, 20A sees when Quaco slips from Abba's back as she leaps limestone—his eyes flung open, his mouth a widening zero; his babycry making it to the other side without him—20A quick-time catching him in her arms, flushed and fever hot. She loosens his rags, takes a rusty horseshoe from around his ankle. It is the same-same one she found back home in the Kingston yard, she is sure. She makes a mental note to check when she wakes up that it's still in her backpack.

closing & opening night bloom;
*   ing distance/ three barks & three*
doors of butter;
*   fly hoof & horse/*
bloom; ing ting

2oA is just about to stir, when Quaco reaches out with little arms; his palms crisscrossed with tracks of the Milky Way, his mouth still at zero point. When she holds him close against her chest, his hair smells of roast corn and woodsmoke and cocoa-tea; she nuzzles her nose there; kisses the top of his head. And, there is something ole-time about him too—a far-away look in his eye as though he has travelled this way before; knows every hill and gully.

He whispers in her ear, "See me here."

her dream membrane [duppy wallpaper] **2.**

··· ꙩꙩꙩꙩꙩ From *the looking-glass; aka, kosmology & ting.*
hello-hello? **hello, mi on the air?** *bass riddim reverbs through rips in the jahlixir/ every now and then we catch a riff of it/ at such times, we are besides ourselves with divine retrograde/*

as for beginnings, we do not know that feeling/ when someone slips through we are the net to catch their fall/ they come with bits of left-over bass/ or every now and then baby-cry/ once a girl came

with a page from a book/ an elderly man had a seed under his tongue// they often come with one

foot of a shoe. we are interested in the things they carry// **did you know mushrooms can grow in space?** *it is not that space of which we speak. push further; lean into the void* **hello? hello? so what does bass riddim turn when it wheels out to neva-neva yard? and what if it**

rides through the crack of a plate? ··· ꙩꙩꙩꙩꙩ *looking-glass; kosmology & ting* **hello? hello? what is the jahlixir? hello?**

··· ꙩꙩꙩꙩꙩ *bless-up, every now and then we catch a riff of it/ at such times, we are besides ourselves with divine retro-grade/ as for beginnings, we do not know that feeling/ when someone slips through we are* ↖↖↖↖↖↖↖ *the net to catch their fall/ they come with bits of leftover bass/ or every now and then baby-cry/once*
a girl came with a page from a book/ an elderly man had a seed under his tongue/ they

often come with one *foot of a shoe/ we are interested in the things they carry/* **did you know that vinyl records spin in space?** *it is not that space of which we speak/ have no*
fear; close your *why-lids/ lean into the void/* **hello? hello?** ··· ꙩꙩꙩꙩꙩ

so what does bass riddim turn when it wheels out the neva yard? and what if it rides through the crack of a— ··· ꙩꙩꙩꙩꙩ *as for endings, we do not know that feeling*

ARKIVE TRIPTYCH

FROM *THE SHANTE ARKIVE*
ZION AWAKE PROJECT (I)

Papilio homeros; Jamaican Swallowtail; also, Shante; aka, *simply boss;*
also, *simply baas*

Dream crossings are excellent spaces of recovery for swallowtails. If you are selected to entah such a dream, it is recommended that you revisit the space again and again for observation and study and to support boss thriving. Sing and big-up *simply boss* the way you root for a favourite sprinter in the dash for the gold, for if they win, you do too.

Know too, there is another (little-known) reason populations are in decline: we have neglected to tell the swallowtail story, and in so doing, have edited them out of consciousness. Your drum and chant will reverb across dimensions and timelines.*

---

* *Kurata's note:*

  1. In the Shante Kollection, simply boss can be communed with strictly in the dream arkive or on location in Jamaican habitats.

  2. Prepare to be observed. Swallowtails can see your true-true colours.

(II)

Neomonachus tropicalis; Caribbean monk seal; also, sea wolf;
aka, *own-mine*

According to official records, Caribbean monk seals are thought to be extinct. In the Shante Dream Kollection they are designated extant, but not extinct, having been sighted by fisherpeople and in warm dream waters.

For after three hundred years of slaughter, monk seals know better than to reveal themselves to humans. These days, they stay low, adapting to below surface conditions and establishing habitat with the underwater spirits of drowned horses and slaves disappeared overboard. For things happen below sea that have never been told. There is wheelin there and turnin; and far-far down past brochure azure, cerulean and indigo, there is a vast dark ink and vortices of voices caught up in such a trumpet of rah-&-glory bottomsea sound as to move earth's axis. And after that, more ink blue, and cobalt and sapphire and a calm-calm wata—velvet and kin to the moon brand new. The monk seals dare not go this far. But the spirits do.

Leap into the salt blue, then, wheelin, wheelin down through the depths, for the arkive is kurated by a connoisseur of bottomless tings—ocean twilight; and sea-cat sky; the reverb of lost riddims; the echoing shades of seawata. Drinks bottles and scandal bags find the fluorescent seafloor; plastic collapsed into spent black lungs.

---

azureceruleanindigoinksapphirecobaltnewmoonblueazureceruleanindigoinksapphire
*cobaltnewmoonblueazureceruleanindigoinksapphirecobaltnewmoon*drinksbox
blueazureceruleanindigoinksapphirecobaltnewmoonblueazureceruleanindigoink
*sapphirecobaltperiwinkleblueazureceruleanindigoinksapphirecobaltnewmoon*bottle
glass*blueazureceruleanindigoinksapphirecobaltnewmoon*sodacan*blueazurecerulean*
indigoinksapphirecobaltnewmoonblueazureceruleanindigoinksapphirecobalnewmoon
scandalbag*blueazureceruleanindigoinksapphirecobaltnewmoonblueazurecerulean*
indigoinksapphirecobaltnewmoonblu–

(III)

Hippocampus erectus; also lined seahorse; aka, *remembrance balm*

Seahorse couples stay together for life. They are what lovers rock is; they dance all night to the songs they play. The male gives birth, having lovingly carried eggs in his pouch, releasing them into red-green-gold fluorescence. Couples twine their tails and sea riddim whine—pure rock away hotness. One-love threatened with extinction.

The sista from 20A dreams of a curly-tail babyfaada. They slow dance in sea moss twilight; take their own sweet time and do not let go; when he releases their children into salt wata, her eyes blink open from the dreamheat, and she—

// wakes with a sudden memory of mail order sea-monkeys. She was eight and had read about them in an uncle's old comics and wanted a family of them so bad but needed $1.25 plus 50¢ shipping in U.S. currency to get them; and probably a U.S. postal address with zip code too. She filled out the order form anyway; kept it in her pillow. She knew about seahorses and imagined sea-monkeys were their kin. And how perfectly American—just add water.

Many years later, on the drive from Newark airport and her eyes adjusting to soon-winter light, there was a gnawing concern she could not yet name—this land of mail order sea-monkeys, this "bowlfull of happiness;" super-rush orders (50¢ extra)//

MANGO-TIME,

& she jumped overboard once

The Greyhound stops at Joplin, the way all pawn shop and lock-&-key and cash loan. No time for a restroom break; and maybe there isn't one anyway. The moon is a piece of water cracker in the sky, and by the time the bus takes off, 20A is asleep, the baby in her arms again. He is warm and smell-sweet. Still, she doesn't want a baby quite yet.

She wants a new pair of boots and a set of gold hoop earrings and a green card, but not a baby. Even in dream, she knows that.

But, she likes the smell of this little one, and there is a sense that she has known him before—

her baby snatched from her arms before the leap—

There's something in the way his tiny toes kick against her stomach; something in the curve of his breath. With dream boots, she traverses the limestone rock, holding him tight; careful not to buck her toe and fall. Fly, nuh? she thinks she hears him say but his mouth is closed, his lips bunched up in no-sound. Look, in the hill and gully distance—an ancestor sleeping under a bush, her head tied with a white cloth. Perhaps the baby will be safe there—in the warm crook of this sudden-auntie's arm.

the sea cold, but merciful—

hear him?

Bits of dream reverb over and over—

baby foot; green card; run, mama, run/
ship wail; back foot; rock-scarf,
run/ sea-baby; curly daddy; run mama, run/

The bus engine roars in REM, and the white cloth on the woman's head comes loose; see how she holds baby Quaco against her chest? 20A placed him there. Did she? New mama caresses him as though he has always belonged to her. And there is something 20A needs to say. She struggles to get the word out; stuck in her throat, it is. *Look*, she finally musters.

The woman hears the faint dream voice behind her—all husky from slumber, and two-worldness. She turns, her eyes searching the hills. 20A wants to speak but the words won't come. Only Quaco sees. *Look*, 20A says again, trying her best to speak louder; and his eyes flit to where she points; his little feet pressing into new mama's belly.

Surprised at how baby's eyes stare, new mama turns again, and this time she sees it—a huge, blak and blue (and—yellow!) butterfly. She squints and slow-rises to her feet, for this strip of yellow has hope in it. A yellow like butter churn; overripe star fruit; lucky bird feather; ackee buss-open. No wait, like a dress she craven fi wear—yellow like the middle of Spanish needle flowers—yes, a yellow-yellow like that. Blak and blue, but a yellow winna fi true.

20A dream-watches in wondament too; thinks to herself she must-must remember this; thinks to herself: *simply boss*. And the butterfly, as if to show what a boss-ooman can do, spin-wheels into the trees and circles back again, sending little shivers across the dreamiverse and a catch-breath to Grammie on her Kingston verandah. Same time, Quaco makes a babysound and kicks his feet harder—and new mama holding him, suddenly lightheaded, catches a vision of wearing a yellow cotton dress in an island future-come-already, her shoulders bare in the hot sun as she waits to cross a traffic street.

It is just before wake-up when 20A window contemplates a drop-down No. 11—all the way at the very edge of the dream. How royal its yellow, but how heavy her feet that cannot move.

mango-time: *girls on swings under trees, chanting the kosmos* [arkive audio/74]

just-so/just-so; Haden/Bombay/Julie/No.11/Plummy/Stringy/Graham//No.11/
Kidney//EastIndian/Black/No.11/Turpentine/Fine-skin/Bastard/No.11/Hairy/
Robin/Beef/No.11/Governor/Hamilton/Parrot/No.11/Ladyfinger/Pint-o-wata/
Parry/No.11/Kent/Green-skin/Long/No.11/Common/Cowfoot/Lucea/No.11/
just-so/just-so; just-so/just-so; just-so/just-so; just-so/just-so; just-so/just-so; just-so/
just-so; just-so/just-so; just-so/just-so; just-so/just-so; just-so/just-so; just-so/just-so;
just-so/just-so; just-so/just-so; just-so/just-so; just-so/just-so; just-so/just-so; just-so/
just-so; just-so/just-so; just-so/just-so; just-so/just-so; just-so/just-so; just-so/just-so;
just-so/just-so; Haden/Bombay/Julie/No.11/Plummy/Stringy/Graham//No.11/
Kidney//EastIndian/Black/No.11/Turpentine/Fine-skin/Bastard/No.11/Hairy/
Robin/Beef/No.11/Governor/Hamilton/Parrot/No.11/Ladyfinger/Pint-o-wata/
Parry//No.11/Kent/Green-skin/Long/No.11/Common/Cowfoot/Lucea/No.11/
just-so/just-so; just-so/just-so; just-so/just-so; just-so/just-so; just-so/just-so; just-so/
just-so; just-so/just-so; just-so/just-so; just-so/just-so; just-so/just-so; just-so/just-so;
just-so/just-so; just-so/just-so; just-so/just-so; just-so/just-so; just-so/just-so; just-so/
just-so; just-so/just-so; just-so/just-so; just-so/just-so/just-so; just-so/just-so;/just-so;
just-so/just-so;Haden/Bombay/Julie/No.11/Plummy/Stringy/Graham//No.11/
Kidney//EastIndian/Black/No.11/Turpentine/Fine-skin/Bastard/No.11/Hairy/
Robin/Beef/No.11/Governor/Hamilton/Parrot/No.11/Ladyfinger/ Pint-o-wata/
Parry/No.11/Kent/Green-skin/Long/No.11/Common/Cowfoot/Lucea/No.11/
just-so/just-so; just-so/just-so; just-so/just-so; just-so/just-so; just-so/just-so; just-so/
just-so; just-so/just-so; just-so/just-so; just-so/just-so; just-so/just-so; just-so/just-so;
just-so/just-so; just-so/just-so; just-so/just-so; just-so/just-so; just-so/just-so; just-so/
just-so; just-so/just-so; just-so/just-so; just-so/just-so; just-so/just-so; just-so/just-so;
just-so/just-so;Haden/Bombay/Julie/No.11/Plummy/Stringy/Graham//No.11/
Kidney//EastIndian/Black/No.11/ Turpentine/Fine-skin/Bastard/No.11/Hairy/
Robin/Beef/No.11/Governor/Hamilton/Parrot/No.11/Ladyfinger/ Pint-o-wata/
Parry//No.11/Kent/Green-skin/Long/No.11/Common/Cowfoot/Lucea/No.11/
just-so/just-so; just-so/just-so; just-so/just-so; just-so/just-so; just-so/just-so; just-so/
just-so; just-so/just-so; just-so/just-so; just-so/just-so; just-so/just-so; just-so/just-so;
just-so/just-so; just-so/just-so; just-so/just-so; just-so/just-so; just-so/just-so; just-so/
just-so; just-so/just-so; just-so/just-so; just-so/just-so; just-so/just-so; just-so/just-so;

20A back at the gate singing *African Starship* with the Dreamgate Dread,
does not see
the overseer in long boots, waiting in the bush,
his machete cut the air—

or Quaco's outstretched arm,
the long-tail butterfly—blak & blue & yellow-yellow, taking flight—

Baby boy's eyes dart
as flocks of birds rush up from the trees—
such a twitter   ing of news and
egg break and feather drop;
new-ma's dress-neck in the overseer's clutch;

only the *whirr-whirr* black birds see
the woman bite the flesh of the overseer's arm,
an act which costs her—

Later, massa records the day's exploits in a journal. He writes with a quill,
shipped from Virginia; the ink is brown rust. *Found that wench, Stella, and
her secret infant.*

So this is how baby Quaco is returned to the plantation. No further records exist—in either dream or wide-wake—until 1807.

hear him?

20A //wakes with a sense that she has lost something, or failed to do
something. She looks all around to be certain her backpack is still there,
and her horseshoe, and notebook. America whooshes by outside the window. She has no memory of the dream, except yellow-yellow and something baby-flight.

QUACO RUNS WITH THE BIRDS

A WEST INDIA SPORTSMAN.

Make haste with the Sangaree, Quashie, and tell Quaco to drive the Birds up to me — I'm ready.

quaco; also cuba; also cue; also cue boy

Check it:

True, not much exists in the arkive on Baby Quaco's early years, however, in both sleep and wide-awake, his cry continues to reverb.

As noted, the very first time he is captured in print-print is in 1807, a young boy pretending to drive birds in the direction of the massa-man relaxing in shade.

The print was a joke, meant to make fun of plantation ways; but sadly, it was hardly an exaggeration. Massa would say, "Quaco, go shit on my behalf," and everyone would laugh; or he would say, "Big boy, fly back to Africa and bring back one of those lions, I need one," and the buckras would stomp feet and sip more rum.

When the ancestors were on the big ships, crossing the Atlantic, they made sport of us that way; made us dance on the deck—to exercise our limbs, they said; but it was also for entertainment—how to do the impossible in chains. On such mornings, the sailors gathered around and hooted and clapped. On the day massa said, "tell Quaco to drive the birds up to me," the boy was sixteen years old. It had been a long day at the mill, feeding cane into massa's iron devil; the heat overbearing. Late afternoon and he sat on a rock to watch the sky as he was wont to do, and dreamer that he was. Overseer pushed him with a boot foot, and Quaco stood up quick then, and made like he was driving the birds.

At first, the birds were annoyed. Who was this boy come to run them? But then, they saw that he was kindred and meant no harm; there was something about the tilt of his head, the reach of his arms—such longing to be taken up into the flock. Instead of heading south, they twittered amongst themselves, surfing air current. Massa watched from half-open eyes, contented and rumfull. As the birds dipped and swirled around the clearing, Quaco followed, his arms reaching higher. He ran behind as the birds rode the air; for they were charting the blueprints of star swirl, and of hurricanes, and of monkey ladder vine, and seed pod whirling on open sea. Something in Quaco remembered that freedom, and yearned for it. He ran and ran behind them, a bird and boy helix. And after a while he forgot about massa, and massa passed out from drink, forgot about him. It was nearly dusk when the birds flew off into the hills, and Quaco soaked with sweat and snot and long eye-wata, returned to his rock under the guango tree.

Some of the people-them thought Quaco was mad or fool-fool, but then again, it was not the first time they had had such thoughts. And then there were some who just stood quiet, watching in the soon-dark, and holding back tears.

The woman, Stella, sniffed and hummed a worry tune. Look-here, her secret infant—the one she held as overseer whipped her—grown all strange ways and far-eye.

Evening came; sunset orange and cut-skinned. And a girl spat—quick, when no one was looking—into the rum caskets; looked around, and spat again. Later, she tied drop-down feather, broken egg-shell and last-laugh in a cloth for Quaco's pocket.

Far-far in the future, 20A looks out at the desert and worry-hums against the bus window, her voice torn around the edges. A contralto mixed of vexation and sorrow, *some a dem a holla;* black birds twitter, and fly, and bend the air.

 At Old Plantation, the motley flock of swifts and swallows came back the next day, and the day after that, and after that. They circled the edges of the cane fields, tracing passage and leaving trails of succour. Such a screeching and cawing of things not seen. Such a dip and dance of it; a knowing that the

air is enough. Quaco studied and watched. And sometimes, after the flocks—exhausted from splendid romp—roosted in their nests, he sat and contemplated the sky; listened to star hum; felt himself moving in it. This is how he learned the workings of wheel-&-come.

mango-time: *girls on swings under trees on the backside of I-finity*
[arkive audio/92]

macca/lovebush/rivariff/blue ⁓ⱱⱱⱱⱱⱱ⁓ ···· *just-so/just-so; just-so/just-so;*
just-so/just-so; just-so/just-so; just-so/just-so; just-so/just-so; just-so/
just-so; just-so/just-so; just-so/just-so; just-so/just-so; just-so/just-so; just-so/
just-so; just-so/just-so; just-so/just-so; just-so/just-so; just-so/just-so; just-so/
just-so; just-so/just-so; just-so/just-so; just-so/just-so; just-so/just-so; just-so/
just-so; just-so/just-so; just-so/just-so; just-so/just-so; just-so/just-so; just-so/
just-so; just-so/just-so; just-so/just-so; just-so/just-so; just-so/just-so; just-so/
just-so; just-so/just-so; just-so/just-so; jusl-so/just-so; just-so/just-so; just-so/
just-so; just-so/just-so; just-so/just-so; just-so/just-so; just-so/just-so; just-so/
just-so; just-so/just-so; just-so/just-so; just-so/just-so; just-so/just-so;
···· ⁓ⱳⱳⱳⱳⱳ⁓ *macca/lovebush/rivariff/blue*:it is untoward to/ talk certain
mysteries/ suffice to say/ we live and breathe/ in an open secret:*macca/*
lovebush/rivariff/blue ⁓ⱱⱱⱱⱱⱱ⁓ ···· *just-so/just-so;just-so/just-so just-so/*
just-so; just-so/just-so; just-so/just-so; just-so/just-so; just-so/just-so; just-so/
just-so; just-so/just-so; just-so/just-so; just-so/just-so; just-so/just-so; just-so/
just-so; just-so/just-so; just-so/just-so; just-so/just-so; just-so/just-so; just-so/
just-so; just-so/just-so just-so/just-so; just-so/just-so; just-so/just-so; just-so/
just-so; just-so/just-so; just-so/just-so;just-so/just-so; just-so/just-so; just-so/
just-so; just-so/just-so; just-so/just-so; just-so/just-so; just-so/just-so; just-so/
just-so; just-so/just-so; just-so/just-so; just-so/just-so; just-so/just-so; just-so/
just-so; just-so/just-so; just-so/just-so; just-so/just-so; just-so/just-so; just-so/
just-so; just-so/just-so; just-so/just-so; just-so/just-so; just-so/just-so; just-so/
just-so; macca/lovebush/rivariff/blue ···· ⁓ⱳⱳⱳⱳⱳ⁓ *just-so/just-so; just-so/*
just-so; just-so/just-so; just-so/just-so; just-so/just-so; just-so/just-so; just-so/
just-so; just-so/just-so; just-so/just-so; just-so/just-so; just-so/just-so; just-so/
just-so; just-so/just-so; just-so/just-so; just-so/just-so; just-so/just-so; just-so/
just-so; just-so/just-so; just-so/just-so; just-so/just-so; just-so/just-so; just-so/
just-so; just-so/just-so; just-so/just-so; just-so/just-so; just-so/just-so; just-so/
just-so; just-so/just-so; just-so/just-so; just-so/just-so; just-so/just-so; just-so/
just-so; just-so/just-so; just-so/just-so; just-so/just-so; just-so/just-so; just-so/
just-so; just-so/just-so; just-so/just-so; just-so/just-so; just-so/just-so; just-so/
just-so;

the trees, the trees-them. plenty, & all of them tall & dark & naked. they
watch me & wait. & listen me when i bawl. for, to who me can turn? *hush*—
the old ones talk like that. i hear it clear-clear, like a betwixt ting that tell
without words. & them times,

me lean into bark & make like me can
disappear inside the honey wata that grow there. *help me find him, nuh?*
& they all stand up straight and quiet on their roots feets.

hush, me hear again from out the betwixt,

& it come to me that Quaco, baby chile mine, fall &
lodge in a place same like that—a betwixt place,
all *hush* & fever & fly-bi-night

between.

hear him?

frequency yard

The dread with the tall locs is there again; he hands her a coconut wata,
fi mi dawta, and a bamboo straw. His smile fills the I-niverse,
sip it slow, and 20A closes her mouth around the coolness,
finishing the wata in exactly the time the earth completes
a mid-way orbit around the sun. She leans into the orbit;
for she too is wheelin, albeit around bits of salt and sugar
and left-over story. Soon as she is done, locsman quick-
time splits the nut in two, *wham!* and they sit together in
the riff of dreaming yard, eating the jelly.

A *story for the I, nuh?* And 20A wonders why this question
for he already sees and higherstands everything. It is just

99

before wake-up and wild pineapple plants push into the riff; and every-where, dragonflies—

this open secret

 A wheelin and a turnin. On some days the birds re-joice; on others, they rebuke and warn. But always, there is wonda in their cry—of cane blossom and woman hum and wood smoke—with each wheel and dip, swift and swallow squawking louder, stretching wonda wider.

Quaco perceives the liberation in their flight, and from henceforth, that's all he can see. Their wings beat the way the wide skirt grand-maddahs wheel at night, their bare feet feeling underground riddim. "No drums, except at Christmas," massa say, but he don't know riddim tings. In moon time, dark feet massage the earth the way birds mate with sky. And so it is, late nights, Quaco raises his arms and opens and closes the air.

The people-them watch him from their corner eye, see how he reaching liberation door. This boy hear when the ancestors talk. They know that any night now, he will up and leave; hope that when he does, he'll come back and free them too.

CANE TRASH

but see-here, how memories collide, explode into trillions of jahlaxies; dust and detritus swirl;ing every which way—yellow cornmeal, hibiscus pollen, a small square of linoleum, a piece of just-born velvet. You collect all the pieces.

In the long nights of the turning of the neva-ending, you breathe the dark and play LPs on rotation; bass riddim takes you to places of open secrets.

You remember a swing under a Julie mango tree; you were seven and would swing there for hours, it seemed. For swinging, like a good bass, suspends time, transports you to places of shoe drop and slip-between. Afterwards, you collected the throw-away seeds from under St Julian and wondered from how far the first one had come, what seas it travelled, and for how long. That summer, you ate star-fruit with your mother as you walked the warm sand at Hellshire. You hurled the tiny seeds into the sea—as far, far out as you could—and she said maybe they would find a home, somewhere. Remember? Hellshire was the last you held her hand. There were noisy-noisy birds up above.

In the humid-hot of the turning of the long days of the evah-lasting, you listen to the radio and smoke a little herbs for the healing of the nation.

Remember this one?—red poinsettias and the house full of aunties and the big yellow bowl with cake mix and a spoon of rum in it. You are twelve and you sniff the left-open bottle and the rum tickles the inside of your nose, rises to the top of your head. You feel a little faint and lean against the kitchen door so you don't fall, for such 40% estate blend takes you back 300 years to a place of cane blossom—high sun and no water; the cane grown tall above your head; overseer's boots coming toward you. Such 40% takes you to a place of noise and churning—late year, and a boy feeding cane into a mill; it is your job to stand beside your friend and quick-quick cut off his arm if it gets stuck in the machine. And-oi, such 40% takes you to a room of heat and boiling where it is your job to test hot sugar with your elbow; you are good for this and nothing else. The room is furious heat and vapor; you faint, and dark molasses drips—

Afterwards, a cake-mix auntie says, These young ones-them, they see visions.

In the loot and the fiah and the Kingston burning, you spin back time and play LPs on rotation.

[*Of wheel & come; or, advice for daring during
waning gibbous sleep*

The carry-go-round pushes, always returning to the
same starting point: wave/rise, eat, sleep; wave/ rise,
eat, sleep; wave/rise, eat, sleep, wave/

Jump off while you can. The trick is to do so right at
the wave. Look-quick, then go. You will see your true-
true self standing on the side, waiting. Leap into her.
You will know when to do it—a wheelin in your belly-bottom; a feeling like when the bass riddim dips.]

Oi,

Oi-oi, to be free of the mill and the grinding. A girl quick-chops Quaco's
finger—just before his hand is taken. The overseer stops the mill; but
only for a bit. Quaco and girl look at each other, afraid. The mill will grind
him to pulp if he is not careful; the girl gets whipped each time she is not
quick. They make a pact to keep each other safe. It is on a day that massa
sends for Quaco to run some foolish errand that another boy takes his
place at the mill. The boy is tired; the machine greedy—the girl quick-
sees—jumps to chop his arm and in the motion the hem of her torn sleeve
catches in the roller, pulling her in, grinding her to—
    They feed her to the dogs.

She was a friend; she and Quaco. He tucked dandelion and fever grass
in her plaits when her ma was sold. Tribulation. They had tasted each
other's sweat.

When Quaco ran with the birds and massa smiled from the corner of his
mouth, she was there. It was she who spat in the rum casks on Quaco's
behalf. And she-same who tied drop-down feather, broken egg-shell and
last-laugh, in a cloth for his pocket.

Oi,
how her feet kicked as the machine chewed.

Look:
bits of blue
thread on the trash
floor; and her hair still caught in the hungry iron;
a piece of ear.

Oi, fallen shoe. Oi rebel spit-phlegm gyal. Oi, last call—*oi!*
Such iron rush, blood-fiah cane-shit hurri-madness will send a boy to
run;ning—

That night,
while protesting with late-squawking birds,

a cleft
in the air
opens—

and Quaco runs and leaps
at the same time
Abba/ jumps

broom/ 56 miles south of Cello with a—

OF QUANTUM RIDDIM;

or, how a slave disappeared from a Jamaica plantation and ended up at a place of flightless birds

The caracara remember when the boy came; he was the first of his kind to arrive there. He appeared on the shore, wet and muddy, having leapt there from a future already-come. The boy was sobbing softly —like soon-come rain—and the caracara pecked around him; picked cane trash from his hair.

It was sun-hot, the island warming itself, the sky a cloudless blue. The caracara were surprised when it stormed. And they were even more surprised when the boy's sob grew to a wail, his face wet with sky.

The caracara argued amongst themselves how to soothe him; they were at wits end about how to stop the wail. He needs his mother, one said. Nah, he needs the old flight feathers, the elders said. Hmm, said the young ones, Those feathers were pre-gifted to someone else. And anyway, looks like he gets around—without them.

They argued late into the night, the storm raging; and still, they could not soothe him.

HEAR HIM?

Quaco-wail reverberated across time, and across rumours of time—mothers heard it and got up in the middle of the night to check on their children/ it could be heard in people's dreams/ in cane fields, early morning/ horses heard it and twitched with remembrance/ swarms of dragonflies rose up, and flew great distances/ someone on a bus heard it/ even now, Quaco-wail inhabits guango trees on a particular corner of the road from Chapleton to Blackwoods/ it is caught in the corners of Kingston rum bars/ and in an old woman's wheezing/ its reverb is lodged in the bent page of a book/ in just-born baby cry/ and a plane taking off—

That storm day, the wail caught fiah and journeyed all the way to a far horizon.

And where are the equations to explain what happened next?

When the wail subsided, Quaco found himself at a gate of no return, three hundred years late. For there were already Black tourists taking pictures there. Later, he would be the person in a photo who no one remembered—a lone figure with bare feet and a feather behind his ear. The place was oddly familiar to him—something about the sea and the impatience of wave-slap against the shore. He wanted to walk and look around, to see if this place had any ripe mango; to see if he might find a little solace there. It was high day and the stars were not visible, but he could still hear them. He was conscious of dry snot on his face and of a bubble still in his throat, and of the low reverb of his wail somewhere in the distance. A woman sat on a wall, eating a mango; a bit of juice collecting in her hand—

[Of wail-&-wheel; or, advice for waxing crescent during wide-awake

Remember this: spiral;ing (aka, wheel-&-come) and circle;ing (aka, betty-run-back) are not to be confused. When in wheel-&-come, one never arrives at exactly the same starting point; it may feel familiar, yes, but you are always most certainly a little more fearless. Hurricanes know this and so do galaxies and black holes; but also, such knowing is in the spirals of shells, in desert tumbleweed; the whorls of night blooming cereus; the cochlea of mama dolphins in deep warm sea; and in Quaco, wailing and bending space.]

of wonda

According to arkival evidence, there are places where Quaco-wail has not yet arrived—light travels faster. His ancient roar still journeys.

Listen careful.

Even now-same, it wheels through the hole in a grandmother's memory; enters the eye of a needle; and the gap between the teeth of a woman selling julie, bombay and stringy mango in the market—her belly-laugh a portal she knew not of. Something there is about an aperture. A flash of bright light—

& you are runnin tings

So it is, Quaco finds himself under the Bombay kindah tree—standing next to one Ms. Z. Sun bright and shine leaf and donkey neigh. And what kind of people these? Black and acting like they own tings. Ms. Z has a hat with a drop-down feather in it. Quaco wants to ask who the bird, and if Ms. Z saw it fly. She has been eating mango and the smell still clings to her. He stands close taking in her mango smell and observing the feather in her hat. No one seems aware of his presence, at least that he can tell. He touches her shoe with his big toe—such a glory of black and blue, and tied so nice with little strings. The man—Colonel, they call him—wears boots and waves a cutlass in the air like it is his to do as he pleases. There is no massa anywhere around. A small girl, with a cloud-puff of soft black hair peeps from behind the tree. Only she can see. She smiles and pinches Quaco on the arm.

A bright flash of light &—

Exposure VII [Kodak Junior Six-16]

What yu name? the girl asks.
   Quaco.
   Qua–?
   Quaco.
   Oh.
   And as she steps around to the other side of the tree, mango leaves pile around her feet. Off to the side, Ms. Z. and the Colonel share jokes about red coats and tree tea and runaway time. The Colonel sticks his cutlass in the ground.
   I go call you Cuba, the girl says. My faadah cut cane there.
   A whirr-whirring makes Cuba look up.
   I know what the birds-them dream, the girl says.

A bright flash of light &—

from the unarkive: what the birds-them dream

wooii,

skye

wooii,

skye   wi go

dweet

wat

if?

w   at

if?

wat

i   f?

blakbird

As the bus passes through Oklahoma, the land flat and dry, 20A thinks to herself, Why am I here in the U.S., anyway? Is it even worth it? I could be at home in Jamaica, sitting under a tree, eating a nice No. 11 mango. I could be shelling peas while listening to Muta on the radio. I could be eating fried fish from Hellshire. I could belong; I could be a citizen; not just some girl-woman on the run, wearing a too-thin coat. It's true, I could also be raking and cussing the leaves in the yard; everyday-everyday, the same thing; my life going nowhere; but so what? If someone watched me from their corner-eye, at least I would know it was because they liked my boss walk, or wanted to tief my purse, but not because they might be from the government with a warrant to deport me.

There on the Greyhound, 20A sees—this America has no end. The flat scrub goes on for miles. Bare rocks; here and there a group of black birds; tumbleweed. The bus forges ahead on the long road.

 At Tulsa, there is a neck-tie man standing by the curb. He looks at his phone; glances in 20A's direction; looks left then right; then turns and goes inside the station. A young woman gets on the bus. She has Milo-with-milk skin and thick black hair tied into a ponytail that reaches the middle of her back. She sits in the empty seat beside 20A, crying softly; wipes her cheeks with her hair. 20A offers a paper napkin from her pocket. She takes it and blows her nose. 20A gives her another and she folds it into a small square, dabs the skin under her eyes. 20A dares not ask what the matter is. The tears keep coming.

Up front, the driver exchanges blackbird stories with a passenger:

> [*The blackbird that flew inside the bus one Christmas morning; the blackbird that followed the bus non-stop from Binghamton to Saint Louis; the blackbird that had a two dollar bill inside its beak; the blackbird that sang,* Chain of Fools.]

The young woman's tears keep coming. 20A thinks she could be about her age. Maybe a little older, but twenties still.

> [*The blackbird at the stop light*. I swear, always the exact-same bird, right by the stop light.]

Her tears wet her jeans. 20A dares not speak. The electric cable wires are lined with blackbirds. Red rock. Red rock. Oh look. Red rock. Red rock. The bus speeds on. 20A rummages in her backpack, finds a pen and an old notebook, and writes: *What's wrong?* Cry-cry looks at the words for a while, then takes the pen.

> [*The blackbird shit behind the driver's seat*.]

the mosquito in their hearts

Her handwriting is loopy, but careful. *I have too many secrets,* she writes. 20A looks through the window and takes these words in for a while, feeling the low rumble of the bus. What secrets? she wonders. Does she have more than me? And why would she share them with a stranger?

Exit signs come and go; tumbleweed bobs along; blackbirds watch as the bus speeds by. Then the answer comes to her: Why not? She will likely never see her again. And too, technically—at least as long as the government does not find her—she does not exist. She could be a mirage. She could be a dream. She could be a figment of the imagination.

> [*Exit*]

> [*Exit*]

At Oklahoma City, 20A writes: *Let's exchange secrets.*

Cry-cry sniffs then, and pauses. She is quiet for a full minute, before she looks at 20A and asks, "Why should I trust you?" It is one of only two times 20A will ever hear her voice. It has barbed wire in it. And salt.

Because I am a fugitive, 20A writes.

This is how 20A and Yolanda Moreno become friends. And this is how they tell each other stories all the way through scrub and desert.

[cough]; also, ewa; also, ikó; also, u̱kwarà; also, kosuk; also, ketiketoo; also—

On the passage from Calabar to Port Royal, Adwoa recalls her name 542 times. Rotten feces, sick heave and parch-throat fill the hull. The baby in the woman's belly beside her is too weak to kick; it waits, fetal and quiet. Remembrance of name is an act of will. In brief fits of Atlantic fever-sleep, Ashante woman discerns swarms of anchovies swirling open-mouthed in the sea; seaweed abloom and free. A curious sea dog follows alongside the ship. It swims the length of the vessel, notes the trepidation therein, takes one look at Ashante woman's dream-awake eyes, then swims away.

[*blue gel ink on lineless paper*]

Y: I think I am losing myself.

20A: Is that why you cry?

Y: I used to fly in my sleep. Now I forget how.

[*Exit*]

[*Exit*]

20A: Can I tell you something?

Y: Yes, all your secrets. Tell.

20A: They are after me.

Y: ?

20A: The govt. I don't have papers.

her dream membrane [duppy wallpaper] 3.

*And you/ you running in a foreign land, the ancestor pant/ ing beside you, is/
and you, you running in a foreign land the ancestor panting behind you/ and
you, running in a foreign land, the ancestor panting before you is/and you, you
running in a foreign land, the ancestor panting behind you is/ and you/ and
you running in a foreign land, the ancestor panting before you is/and you, you
running in a foreign land, your ancestor panting behind you is/and you running
in a foreign land your ancestor panting before you is/you running, running,
running, in   a foreign land, land, land, your ancestors panting behind
you are/and you, you running in a foreign land, the ancestor panting behind
you, is/and you, your running in a foreign land, the ancestor panting before
you is/and you, you running in a foreign land, the ancestor breathing behind
you is/and you,   your running in a foreign land, the and you, you running
in a foreign land, the ancestor calling behind you is/and you, you running in a
foreign   land the ancestor calling—hear her?—is/ and you, you running in a
foreign land the ancestor calling   ·   and you, you running in a foreign land,
the ancestor   calling behind you is/ and you, you running in a foreign
land, the descendant calling before you is/ and you, you running in a foreign
land, the descendant calling   you is descendant/you, yes you, running before,
hear her? you running in a foreign land, the ancestor running beside you, yes,
you—you dreaming in a foreign land, you running and dreaming; and and running and dreaming and dreaming and running, and running and dreaming and
dreaming and running and running and dreaming and dreaming and running
and running and dreaming and dreaming and running and running and
dreaming and dreaming and move by whenever is, and running and dreaming
and dreaming and running and running and dreaming and dreaming and running and running and/ hear her? the ancestor is walking behind you; yes you,
you in a land; the ancestor walks beside you; hear her? she runs beside
you/she calls behind you/she cries before you hear? the ancestor is
beside you; the ancestor is dreaming beside you; gives you; beside you;
the ancestor is dreaming beside you; the ancestor breathes beside you; hear?
hear her? the ancestor is calling; the ancestor laughs; hear? the ancestor is
breathing beside you; is dreaming beside you; the ancestor is beside you; is
besides herself with—hello? we're on the air.*

[*blue gel ink on lineless paper*]

Y: Me, I have papers. But, no memories—worse than no papers. Born in Cuba. Walked from Venezuela.

20A: Is that make you cry?

Y: I used to make pollen in my sleep. Now I have insomnia.

    [*Hey, folks. Next stop, rest stop—*]

20A: Is that make you cry?

Y: 5 years. Many borders. You walk from where?

20A: Jamaica. On water.

    [*Exit*]

    [*Exit*]

    [*Exit*]

    [*Exit*]

Y: Did you know that 300 mill. years ago Jamaica and Cuba and Venezuela touched?

20A: Why you cry so hard?

    [*Exit*]

Y: Did you know that scientists have grown plants from very old seeds?

20A: But why you cry?

[*Exit*]

Y: I found very old seeds in a book. In a dream. Now I have insomnia and cannot get them.

20A: Is that make you cry?

Yolanda wipes her face with her hair, twists in her seat and turns her back. A strange one, she is. 20A goes back to watching shrub and rock. Her mind wanders to her Kingston yard and to the hibiscus there; yellow pollen floating on water; duck ant wings on the verandah floor; her Grams fallen on the back stoop, her glasses smashed on the concrete. A faint riff of Gram-voice on the phone–*duck ants can travel underground a mile or more.** The rumble of the bus makes her eyes heavy.

   can travel underground a mile or more—Gamma sits on the verandah; watches the
duck ants nest on the neighbour's mango tree. From how far did they travel to come eat
down her house? Duck ants love to devour books. Should we hold it against them?

2oA //awakens in her dream to a swarm of dragonflies; a host of irides-cent blue not-there-but-there riding the bend of a riva. The dragonflies dance over rock and sand and eel and mullet; riva and fly calling out to each other above the roar of the dreamiverse; they dip-and-turn and 2oA stands still, feeling the dragons do a helix around her waist. Passed hill and gully and limestone, baby Quaco cries out from the far-far edge of the dream, just as the swarm disappears up riva.

hear him?

kuratorial ephemera

You remember when your mother died, how a dragonfly came and pitched on the window; how it stayed
there for hours and hours and would not move. You
knew it was her come back to see you; come to say
hello and good-bye. It was blue-blue like the cotton
dress she liked best. Dragonflies are that way.

When at last it flew away, it never came back—

Mama? Since then, you record dragonflies wher-
ever they are found—along streams, in abandoned
thoughts, in slithers of memory. The records are as
fleeting as the dragons themselves. Look quick—a
swarm crossing sea, carrying ministration, their wings
beat beneath the chorus in your ear—of iron wheels
turning; a cough submerged underwater; pregnant
stars in labor; a long wail—

At Amarillo, Yolanda turns around and writes in the notebook.

Y: It was my favourite colour.

20A: What was?

Y: Amarillo. I used to feel amarillo inside.

20A: You can feel it again. But what makes you sad so?

Y: Sometimes we disappear.

20A: Only on paper.

Y: I like your little book. It is without line and law.

20A: :)

Y: See how crooked? We write crooked.

20A: You neva answer me.

Y: Did you know there is evidence of prehistoric insect pollination?

20A: Off topic.

Yolanda smiles a small broken smile then, and for the first time 20A catches a glimpse of her teeth, a praying mantis tattooed in the groove above her lip. The bus pulls away and 20A leans into her seat. She is so hungry now but better to save her $12 and 5 cents. The desert makes her think of a bedtime story, *and she lived ever and ever after.* But this land is ever and ever, with no after. She puts her hand against the window. Perhaps something out there will catch the shadow of her palm and find its lines. The rocks are witness.

[*Exit*]

Y: They have a soundtrack? Your dreams?

20A: Bass riddim. It's how my heart beats.

[*Exit*]

Y: I envy your sleep. I watch your eyelids how they jump.

20A: Sleep delays hunger. Tell me a secret. Secrets are food too.

[*Exit*]

[*A woman left her baby on the bus one night; right there on the back seat. Drove all the way to Gallup before I heard it cry. Can you believe it? All the way to Gallup.*]

[*Exit*]

Y: The best secrets are the ones inside dreams. You remember them? Your dreams?

20A: Only now and then. I found a very old letter in a dream once. Under a stone.

[*Exit*]

[*Exit*]

Y: Sometimes I think our dreams are endangered. What did the letter say?

[*Exit*]

20A: Never figured out how to read it. But check this: in dreams, I know

I am dreaming.

Y: So lucky. I used to have a recurring dream. The one where I found the very old seeds.

20A: Hibiscus?

Y: No. That's the pollen I knew how to make. Can I tell you a secret?

20A: Waiting.

   [*Exit*]

Y: Sometimes, I want to go back the way I came. Like when you walk back to find something lost. You know? Maybe then, I would find it again—the dream, and the thing in it I didn't finish.

20A: Return is in our blood. I want a No. 11 so bad.

Y: No. 11?

20A: A mango. A long time ago, they came on a ship and were all numbered.

Y: 11. Like the two sticks in amarillo.

BEING AN INSINUATING WENCH

There is an old man calling Abba with his finger. He is from the-already and is a dreamer too. Dreamer that she is, 20A recognizes this right away; she, dreaming on a Greyhound through highway-night. Abba, searching the sky for signs, sees neither of them.

With silver hair and blue shirt and cup of cerasee tea, he has journeyed all the way from the year 1988 where it is hurricane season and a furious rain is falling on his St. Thomas parish house. He has boarded up his windows and gone to bed to ride out Gilbert. And there, he has come across Abba—wandering in unfamiliar woods—Quaco-cry in the treetops, but no Quaco. The man sees 20A too—but only in a corner-eye dream-ether way, the same way she is only half aware of Yolanda next to her, her chest rising and falling with little sobs.

20A's //eyes open as the bus swerves to avoid a tire in the middle of the road. It is cold and she pulls her jacket close. Yolanda quiet now, has her eyes closed, but is not sleeping. She has left a new note in 20A's book.

Y: Mangoes are messy.

> [*A woman hid in the toilet once. Yep. Never did find out what she was running from.*]

20A: That's why I like them.

the kurata of dreams & of small acts

There was a day, after she died, that you found a dead pea dove and brought it home. Your aunties scolded you; made you dash it away. Your dream that night was filled with bird-feather. The feathers fell from a place that was beyond the sky—a place filled with eye-wata steam and bits of belly laugh and lost-&-found respect, ephemera in need of refuge. The bird-feather dream was the first time you fell in love with sleep-wake.

In your dreams now, you find feathers and put them in books for safekeeping; you find the end notes of tunes on the radio; and bits of girl-scream caught in wind; you keep words without sound under your tongue—ones that have fallen on deaf ears; or gone unsaid and which might be useful for the here-already and the yet-to-come because don't they are both happening at the same time? In your dream you collect footsteps for redistribution across time, because there are moments when all a body needs is just an extra half-leap to cross the border, escape the slammed door, the barking dog, the turning mill or swerving car; you collect chips of dreamity people forget—that is, you find theirs in yours—and hold sacred the memories that nearly got erased or the bits of voice that slipped underground; you keep that too, just because.

In your dream you make note of a brown dog twitching its ear, a butterfly rubbing its wings together, and a hand turning the page of a book because such small acts should never be taken for granted.

SHE MIGHT HAVE CHANGED HER NAME

abba; *of kin/etic sky &*

Look: a patch of sunshine and a tree with tiny leaves on it. A stream runs near, with fish. Abba takes off a shoe and tries to catch one. It swims out through the open toe. She cups her hands and tries again, but the fish are too quick. She stands, dizzy from hunger and fatigue, and has a flash of girl-chile remembrance—a swarm of dragonflies rising ahead, following the bend of a riva; and as they advance, a feeling—for one moment—that she was part of the swarm; the air all mist and shimmer light.

She steadies herself; leans against a rock—a *hush* around it. How this place is full of kin. Sometimes Abba feels a breath at her neck. And a muffled voice that says, *run.* And still sometimes, she hears Quaco cry—his voice faint-faint, caught up in the screech of birds passing overhead. She is sure it is him—his see-mi-here cry filled with rain and cane trash and long-journey breeze—but the earth is all turned around and wrong-side now and the baby-voice disappears as soon as she tries to follow it.

It is on a day that Baby Quaco cries, that she finally sees the St. Thomas man sitting under a tree.

abba; *hush &* [arkive audio Transcript/4]

See-here, a grown man talking to the air. right
away, i know he not from this coldment place—
i can tell. the way he say, evenin miss. a home voice—from the other side of the leap. but this man different still. look, pants all soon-night blue and
        careful-stitch, & shoes—with
thick bottoms & a turnin, turnin
ting on his wrist, like the clock in mistress thiefen house.

i say, evenin & he say, i been waiting for you to turn
& see mi. so i say, what's that on yu wrist, look like white people tings?
& he say, take it, everyting that happen is at the same time it happening
        anyway.

137

this man talk strange but i don't fraid him. i think he can help me. so i say,
i lookin mi baby—him name Quaco. & he say, the last i heard he was
chasing birds. a sista dreaming and riding a bus saw it.
yu talk like yu mad, i say. &
same time i say that, the calling birds come
back again & them stretch cross the sky, caw-caw, caw-caw, but
underneath that, maa-maa, maa-maa &

with dry cane trash catch up in it—

hear him?

maa-maa & [arkive audio transcript/5]

the man put the wrist clock in my open hand. a little stick inside it turn
around & around. it look like a freedom ting, i say. no, is a slave ting, he
say.

i want to open it to see what's inside. i try & try but it
don't budge & the little stick inside neva stoppin. what's this zick-zick,
zick-zick?

some people hear it all day, he say.

i don't need no more trouble; uh-uh.
lost mi baby & mi freedom paper too. leaped a leap &
landed here. feels like years i in these woods.

hurricane mad outside, he say, everything wheelin,
wheelin. let me check the windows & mi two goats-them;
when i come back, maybe we can jump
together, see where it leads.

& just like that, he walk away.

i hold the wrist clock in my hand & shake-it shake-it &
knock it with a stone &
fling it &

rain begin to fall
& hot eye wata.

rhaatid, she said

The man leaves the dream, just as 20A's head nods forward and she jolts //
awake again. Yolanda still has her eyes closed, and the bus driver is talking
to a passenger up front about tumbleweed and yucca and blue grama grass.
20A likes this word, *tumbleweed*, and thinks to herself that she and it could
become friends. They could hitchhike the country, she and it, and see
where they end up. Maybe even hitch on a cargo ship and cross seas. She
knew a man in Jamaica once who, tired of street and gun and hungry-belly,
hid on a ship docked in Kingston harbour and sailed all the way to Barce-
lona. The crew found him, of course, and roughed him up and sent him
back, but for what it's worth, he crossed sea at the bottom of a ship. He
said for weeks the sea rocked and roared and there was no day and no night
and he slept on board-floor between crates which leaked something pus
and when he dreamed, there was wailing and bawling and iron chains in it.
The ship-bottom had a vomit smell too, full of thirst and headache and a
feeling same-like motherless chile. This is how he knew they had reached
middle-Atlantic. Whenever he told the motherless part, his eyes steamed
up and he looked away, for story had it, he grew up in deep concrete jungle
and was raised by left-alone youth like himself, and sometimes by stray
dogs, and sometimes by a one-drop riddim and the kindness of cemetery
duppies. But jesus-god, the neighing of mad horses on that ship. People
asked: The neigh was dream reverb or true-true horses on the ship? But
he didn't know. The sea rocked and rocked and soon he neighed too. One
night in a dream, a rebel mind came over him and he neigh-wailed and

leapt—all the way overboard—into the wata, its roaring swallowing him; he and sea making conspiracy. He knew he and it were in conspiracy because of how every part of the sea was every part of him, the same-same oneness, swaying and spawning. Wide and sergeant as the Atlantic-self, it was he who ruled and moved the ship and the direction of it. It was he who was captain of the big wata. This is how he remembered his own true self and returned to Jamaica to live strong and simple, driving taxi and telling bottom-sea tings.

His passengers called him Seaman; and some of them asked to hear the dream story again and again. When he got to the bit about wailing and riding the roar of the wata they always said, "Rhaatid"—real sof and real low, as though they had somehow forgotten, but now remembered their own true-self, it all happening to them in bottom-sea too.

20A remembers driving in Seaman's taxi with her Gramma; and how when he got to the jump, Gramma began to sniff but tried to hide it and coughed instead. He dropped them at their gate off Sunward Drive and her Gram said, Plenty thanks, Seaman. And he smiled and said, Beg you a mango? And they picked some of the No. 11 hanging over the fence.

The next time they rode with him, he told the story of how No. 11 travelled long ways to get to Jamaica—on a ship, he said. And how all the mangoes on the vessel were numbered, the way how all the hairs on our head are numbered, but this one number stuck. Number 11 is a special-special number, he said. And 20A remembers how she asked, "Mr. Seaman, did the mangoes dream?" And everyone laughed. But after, they all looked through the window and were quiet.

20A thinks to herself that she could be like tumbleweed and hitch ride after ride and see America, and that then, it just might be worth it, all this American no-citizen botheration to rah. When Yolanda opens her eyes, 20A writes in her notebook:

20A: There was no one at the airport to meet me and I was afraid.

20A/window arrived at Newark in a cream soda dress and with shoes that
hurt. It was her best dress, everything she had taken was her best, and her
only. She had a zip-up, no-wheels suitcase with the horseshoe inside, and
her clothes, and the book of devotions from Grams, and the Zora book.
She also had bun and cheese and a roasted breadfruit. She was to meet
her cousin, Velma (who everyone called Vee) at the airport, Vee who had
helped file the papers for her visitor's visa. 20A could spend a few weeks
until Vee's boyfriend came back from deployment overseas, Vee said. But
she could not spend longer than the few weeks because there would be
nowhere to accommodate her after that. "Come here and get away for a
while; keep me company till Wes gets back." Vee said. And too, there was
the promise of a job, cleaning houses. 20A needed money.

Vee worked in a pharmacy, developing film. She lived in a one-room above
a laundromat and planned to marry her American soldier, Wesley, soon
as he came back from Germany. She called 20A in Kingston sometimes;
told her stories about Wes (and Wes and Wes) and NJ, and how when no
one was looking, she flipped through customer photos before filing them
in the pick-up bin. Sometimes, people left reels of film and never came
back to pick them up, she said. She always felt sad when that happened,
like they left a part of themselves behind. Those were the ones she liked to
flip through most—bits of life forgotten—the hand holding a baby's foot;
the old woman in the hospital bed (maybe her last photo); the cat in the
middle of the road.

The day 20A arrived at Newark airport, Vee was not there to pick her up.
20A waited outside the automatic doors, cars and taxis coming and going;
her feet burning her in the too-tight shoes; her cream soda dress sticky
under her arms; her phone no use. It was getting dark when a woman
tapped her on the shoulder and said, "Velma's cousin?" A Jamaican voice.
And then, "I'm here to pick you up."
    "And your name?"
    "Peaches—a friend of Vee."

Peaches wore dangling heart earrings and a broad smile. The trunk of her car smelled like synthetic flowers and was full of bags of lipstick and hand lotion and bath soap. I sell Avon, Peaches said. There was barely space for the zip-up suitcase. It felt odd riding in a stranger's perfume bottle car, but Peaches made conversation and was pleasant enough. She said Vee had been trying to reach 20A; said she left for Germany—her boyfriend bought her a surprise ticket. Don't worry, Peaches said. Vee says you can stay in her apartment and leave when you're ready. She'll pay the rent. Peaches honked her horn at the taxi in front; yelled something out the window.

I heard of a woman who spent a whole month living at LaGuardia, Peaches said. No one came to pick her up and she didn't speak English and was too scared to leave. But 20A was barely listening, so angry she was at Vee.

Peaches kept talking as the highway rushed by—big bill boards and over-sized trucks and exits and exits and exits—

Land of mail order sea-monkeys, this "bowlfull of happiness;" super-rush orders (50¢ extra) /

20A spent the summer and fall in Vee's apartment. Vee never came back and only sent two month's rent; the lease ran out. 20A knew how to sew and when a worker went missing, the man who owned the dry-cleaning/ laundromat/alteration shop downstairs gave her some work. I pay you under the table, he said. She sewed hems and zippers on a Singer by the window, quick-quick; pressed the dry-clean clothes, on her feet/on her feet; delivery door swinging; hot in summer; cold in winter; machines going round/going round, fiah and turbulence; swept the trash and lint; and the dutty toilet, cleaned it; fed the cat, the poor soul; if asked to work late or weekends there was never anything extra, but she did it and shut up. It was enough to take over the lease and buy ramen noodles and sardines and crackers and send home a little money to Gramma; Grams had a fall at the back stoop and needed to pay for hip surgery. O Grams. When the news came that 20A had failed all her school subjects, she weighed her options, and stayed.

Y: Do you wish you went back?

[cough]; also, ewa; also, ikó; also, ụkwarà; also, kosuk; also, ketiketoo; also—

The sea rocks the ship and the belly woman vomits against Adwoa's neck; and the bell rings; and Ashante woman coughs; and the girl-chile next to her speaks in an unknown tongue. Up on the deck a bird hitches a ride, exhausted from flight; ship sails brace rain and squall. There are rats on board and five barking dogs. And a horse strung up in a sling. The people bawl and call; they cuss in every language; and too, they pray. Someone dreaming in the future hears; someone dancing in the past hears too. I'm here, the future ones say—I won't forget you; cuss louder the ancestors say, we are dancing you into existence. Adwoa hears a horse through the din; it dreams of galloping the Atlantic in a herd a thousand strong, flying-fish and eel and marlin and sargasso weed uprising beneath their hooves.

SILVER BUTTONS FROM
DEEP SEA-BOTTOM

sound check:

Bang sound; big sound; sweet chune a play, and the Kingston brown dogs will not be outdone; they bark into the wee hours, long-side the sound system—

nothing like a good dog fight; found sound; ruff it up or shut it up; muzzle-free zone barking; first dogs; last dogs; this is how we bruk it up/

Full moon a-shine and the brown dogs bark our history; for their ancestors were here from way-way back. Some of them companions to Taino, they barked when three ships appeared on the horizon; good souls they were—they did not know badmind. Some ran to the hills when cares-of-life shook over; ate anole lizard and drop-down guava and learned to keep their bark quiet. Later, others came on ships—sniffing deck for dead rats; licking at the feet of Africans in chains. And look today-self, a brown stray at the corner of Hagley Park and Omara has a flash of memory of a buried ancestor, surprises itself with big barksound; stops and perks its ears up, wondering at its own howl. Everyone of us, dog and human, has a mastiff relative somewhere in our DNA. Oye, long-tailed conquistador; maddened ancestor, what is your story?

system check in the heart of Kingston; check out the bass line; see wha it a gwaan wid—

nothing like a good dog fight; found sound; ground hound; ruff it up or shut it up; muzzle-free zone barking; first dogs; last dogs; this is how we bruk it up/

Weary of heat and bark, a little dog stands at a gate. It waits for morning when an old woman will come with a bag of water crackers; toss some through the iron grill; whisper, "Look here, mi Jesus."

bark

20A closes her eyes and imagines she is riding a greyhound's back. In her magination, she is a small girl in a torn dress; she leans forward and hugs the hound's neck. She and the hound are silent compatriots, itinerant and hitchhiker moving without sound; 20A rides the way egrets ride cows; starfish ride sea turtles; barnacles ride whales. She thinks to herself that Yolanda—fervent earthstorian that she is—would say living things have been doing this for millions of years, for more years than stars in the sky. And 20A—furtive fugitive that she is—likes the idea of being connected to pre-herstoric stowaways. This is how she nods off to sleep and makes peace with a hungry hound; helps it remember another use for its gifts.

Having abandoned its scent for slaves, the greyhound leaps through the expanding dream—

>   *dogbark/ whirr;ing/*
>   *tumbleblak/ weed—*

to a place where dream;ing and jahlixir are one.

20A feeds it water crackers.

memory check:

The brain's hippocampus is shaped like a curly tailed seahorse. Inside our seahorse, memories are stored—kept safe, right there in the curl. And too, the little seahorse helps us criss-cross spaces and places. If you find your way back to yard, give thanks to your horse. And since time and space are twin, might we also say, seahorse helps us navigate time? Something there is about a curl-up tail. Seahorse people entwine and whine and share sea-bottom tings.

Check this: when Seaman dreams of leaping into wata, his seahorse activates. And when he tells the dreamstory to his taxi riders, theirs do too, all salt wata and remembrance balm.

Check this: 20A's Grammie sits and waits on the verandah. Today, bless her, she has forgotten that 20A will not be coming back. Hallelujah—she whispers to herself; My grans is on her way. She thinks 20A is returning from America this afternoon-self; and she has even made saltfish fritters and fried-over breadfruit. The food is covered up on the stove under the kitchen towel printed with a map of Jamaica. There is also a bowl of No. 11 mangos—20A's favourite. Gramma sings songs of redemption as she waits. The plane must be late.

Remember;ing is a mix-up; is a re-mix; is a—

Gramma forgets because she is also busy remembering. The memories so far, and so deep and trance, that there is no more here-so left. There on the verandah, the neighbours' dogs barking, she has a fleeting sensation of running, through trees, her legs scratched up from macca bush and john-crow vine. Her heart beats quick-quick and she breathes heavy-heavy; her head dizzy. Something flits—black and butter-yellow/black and butter-yellow—

Grammie takes a nutmeg from her pocket. After this, there is only one left. The next-door neighbour woman gave her three and said, Anytime you feel your heart-pain boom too hard, pinch little bit and rest it under your tongue. Grammie quiets herself and the feeling passes; she looks out towards the gate, listening for her grans, sweet girl that ran off with mangoes in her bag. Different and own-mind just like her dead mama, and always with her head in a book.

there was a ting they used to boil in the country—search mi heart; the plane must be late. long-wing fly, so black and yellow-yellow, how yu follow me? but see-here, mi grans soon-come with her butterfly book and remembrance psalms. those dogs, eh? what a mix-up ting.

[blue gel ink on lineless paper]

20A: I wish I had another good book. A No. 11 mango, and a good book. Want to know another secret? In Jamaica, I used to steal books from a store in town. I read them, then took them back. The cashier guy knew, and helped me do it. I knew him from my auntie's church. You think God's eyes were watching?

Y: Small acts of noncompliance committed for the love of, or on behalf of great art always have God's approval.

20A: You sound old sometimes. Not old-old, but old.

Y: In the dream I (used to) have, I am old.

Yolanda pulls a black t-shirt from her backpack and buries her face in it; rocks side to side.

> [*Once a boy recited poems from Winslow to LA—young kid maybe sixteen, seventeen; the words just flew—like crows—out his mouth. And oh, I only wish that I could weep just once again—that line! I swear; I swear I'll always remember that line. And jeez, how his voice broke.*]

20A: Would you like to just talk now?

Y: No. The sound of my voice makes me sad.

20A: His name was Tyrell, but they called him Tuff.

out of the blak and blue

The dread at the dreamgate is still there. He sits on a rock reading a book from a future already-come.

This time, the locs stretch crossways—each in an opposite direction—all the way into I-finity. 20A has a thought that one could walk a tight-rope on such dreadnificent locs, stepping careful across the deep. If you fall, no fear—the jahlixir is there—inhale and fill your lungs, take in the blue-blak, exhale a neva ending.

Bless-up dawta, the dread says as he hands her a mango—a beautiful St. Julien that holds a riddim inside. She sits quietly next to him, eating and licking her fingers. Bless-up, she finally replies, not certain whether it has been two seconds or two hundred years.

I need your help, 20A says. I have a friend who no longer sleeps and who cannot dream.

BETWIXT & BETWEEN

[*Of insomnia; or advice for waxing gibbous during wide-wake*

Consider this: The Jamaican swallowtail, *simply boss,* dreams inside its dream. And, awakes inside its awakened self. These butterflies are a materialised frequency riff from an elixir most of us do not see. The dread at the dreamgate calls it jahlixir—the arkive of the unarkivable—aka., kosmology and ting.

simply boss is the largest butterfly in the Western hemisphere because at one time, back when we understood that we and the swallowtail were of one and the same riff, we dreamed it so; and it too, dreamed us. In those days, there was no such thing as insomnia because sleep and wide-awake were the same dream; and dream and sleep were the same wide-awake. Consider that perhaps—even now—there is no such thing as insomnia.

Do not collect these butterflies. And do not disturb their habitat. For then, there will be less dream in the wide-awake and less wide-awake in the dream.]

out of the blak and blue

2OA: What is the jahlixir made of?

DREAMGATE DREAD: Riddim & ting.

2OA: But what is the jahlixir made of?

DREAMGATE DREAD: Jahrithmetics.

2OA: Just tell me nuh, what is the jahlixir made of?

DREAMGATE DREAD: Coconut wata, good fi mi dawta

2OA: No joke, Ras. What is the jahlixir made of?

DREAMGATE DREAD: I&I&I&I&I&—

2OA: Is it real?

DREAMGATE DREAD: What is real?

invasive species [blue gel ink on lineless paper]

Y: Did you know that insects populated the earth millions of years before flowers?

2OA: Is that your secret?

Y: Not really. Just something I like to think about. First in flight too.

2OA: In dreams there is no first and no last. No before and no after.

    [*Exit*]

[*Exit*]

Y: Then how did we all drift apart?

[*Exit*]

[*Exit*]

[*Exit*]

Y: Did you know that Russian thistle came here by chance? Now it's an invasive species. Kinda badass.

20A: Really though?

[*Exit*]

20A: This feels like school. Us writing. I used to pass notes to Arlene Livingston in grade six. That's how I found out there was the tip of a girl's baby finger back of her fridge. She kept it there from a schoolyard fight.

Y: Was that a secret?

20A: No one knew except me.

[*You know what the whoosh of the door reminds me of?*]

[*Exit*]

[*Exit*]

[*Exit*]

Y: The bus is limbo. Telling doesn't count.

[*Exit*]

[*Exit*]

out of the blak and blue

Tell me a secret, 20A says to the Dreamgate Dread. And something about her words feels half talking to him, half writing to Yolanda. Her eyelids flutter, and she is vaguely aware of the bus engine, and of Yolanda fidgeting beside her.

And too, she is aware of how dreams kiss like a meeting of seas; swirl in sync with distant galaxies; touch the event horizon of stories Grammie once told: how she ran from home once, then flew with a butterfly—

The Dreamgate Dread contemplates 20A's request, then says, Don't let dem fool yu with straight lines.

2/wheelin, wheelin

The doctor takes his sounding trumpet from around his neck and listens to Grammie's heart. Her heart goes pit pat pit pat very fast then very slow, very fast then very slow. There is a churning, churning of the blood. It whooshes and whooshes. When she dies it will be said that she had a bad heart condition but was a fine woman with a good heart.

The clock at Half Way Tree has stopped again. Someone made a fire inside and now it's broken. The clock face is melted, like a Dali painting.

Galaxies whirl with an arm outstretched; a wheel-&-come born of the music inside the jahlixir. Entah, if you will. Feel the air; inch your feet; now dip and spin. If you wheel long enough, you might find yourself dancing the dance Queen Nanny danced when she and the ancestors defeated the

British; and sounded the abeng and wheel even longer, and you might remember the one you danced when you were three and knew the algoriddims of stars; dance some more and who knows? As your feet massage the
earth, you might bring caracara back into existence. Keep going.

Hear the drums from across the hill? Sea levels are rising and

simply boss wheels her skirt in a figure eight, swallowtail skankin:

> *flocka   swallow s on the turn*
> > > *table/   mash up the place but*
> *watch*
>
> *wheh yu walk/*
> > *in a world   that's changin/*
> > > *gotta stay boss.*

Quick-quick. There is only half nutmeg left.

flight check:

 The 1758 snow goose flew with its feet tucked under. It
landed in Jamaica and stood on a rock on one foot, the
river nearby brown as quill ink. Snow goose was off
course a little, perhaps. Or perhaps, it meant to find a
respite from hunters. It flew down the Mississippi then
caught a riff of warm air that brought it to this far place. The riff had a
humming in it. And running in it. And it had a bass riddim from a future
come-again, and from a past come-back. And it had weeping and wailing
in it. And babysound and duppy laugh too. The snow goose stuck its neck
out—because that's what geese do—and flew. It would be many days
before it landed, the warm respite short-lived by gunshot—

Quaco standing under the kindah tree hears the shot, and jumps. Grammie sitting on her veranda jumps too. The sound wakes her from a dream of riding a bus; a long-legged dog racing alongside it, trying to keep up. Grammie pushes her hand in her pocket, feeling for nutmeg; looks out towards the gate where a little dog wags its tail for more water crackers.

What a bam bam. Sea-level rising and people hoarding flour, the radio says. On FM, there is talk of hurricane season: stock extra water; board up your windows; buy your medicine; secure your roof. Maybe hurricane has delayed the plane.

what happen to that butterfly gyal? that long-time gyal. neva mind, I'll paint the walls yellow; a little colour strengthens the heart.

a bang

//wakes the sleeping passengers. The bus has a flat.

[*Sorry, folks. The next ride comes from Phoenix.*]

What the rah, 20A says out loud and at the sound of her voice, Yolanda looks at her as if she committed cardinal sin. 20A smiles and puts her hand over her mouth. The toddler in the back begins to fuss for chips and the European backpackers stand up and walk to the front. There is wind and dust. The driver turns the engine off, then on again. The backpackers want to exit and take photos of the dust, but the wind is too strong; they decide not to.

[*Saw a tire fly off a truck and roll across the road once. That was the day, honest to God, when some kinda ghost girl got on the bus. Heard her laugh when the tire flew.*]

Y: Dust has all our ground up stuff in it. Did you know dust falls from space?

20A: No wonder back home I am always sweeping. If we could eat dust we would neva hungry.

arkive of the imagi⊚nation

Dream and imagi⊚nation are two first cousins; they live on separate shores and don't like to be confused. The keeper of the dreamgate is the long-locs dread, while the keeper of magi⊚nation is a wheelin, wheelin held up by an elaborate and expanding jahrithmetics.

The genius of both tends to go unrecognised. They are the outside cousins not invited to the table—they know too many secrets, have no respect for other people's time or space, and have a tendency to bring up random stories. We are a little afraid of them.

Imagi wheels in the void behind ampersands; or sometimes, in that place between your eyebrows where the feeling of the nation spins on a turntable. Some say, it is the riddim ting that fuels the jahlixir.

Look slantways from your corner-eye and listen with your foot-bottom; keep your palms open and become what is found there.

Maybe, magi⊚nation is an act of revolution.

Maybe, wi magi⊚nation is all there is.

ARKIVAL INK

in the between time of the meanwhile;

the dust swirls; and the wind shakes the bus; and the toddler fusses; and the driver tells stories; and the old woman prays; and the Amish eat sandwiches; and the drunk sings; and the European backpackers decide to hike; and the guitar guy opens his guitar case—it is full of dead moths—and Yolanda sniffs; and 20A sleeps because sleep makes you forget, and remember.

out of the blak and blue,

 the dread at the dreamgate gives 20A a Bombay. She was hoping for a No. 11; still, she takes the ripe fruit with bottom-heart thanks, holds it careful with both hands. One inhale and she knows that this mango is of the highest realms; it is alpha and omega. She eats the flesh and the skin too, and sucks the seed until it is white.

One time, a Malagasy dawta hid a seed in her hair, the dread says. It stayed there, all the way cross the middle passage. That was the first one to come, but later there were more—from India and ting because that's where the motha seed was dreamed.

20A pauses, imagining the woman with her plenty hair, the Bombay seed hidden in a knot on top of her head.

Is the kinda ting you only come to higherstand here-so—dream side, he says.

And 20A sees the woman pretend to scratch her scalp; the remembrance of glossy leaves in her eyes.

We came from Madagascar too?

But of course. You neva know?

And with that 20/A coughs and blinks //awake, the wind shaking the bus.

[*Listen up, folks. Bus from Phoenix is delayed. But they're sending someone to fix the flat.*]

The elderly woman across the aisle begins to cuss and pray. She reminds 20A of her Grammie—her plaits tied up in a scarf and with ankle socks over her stockings. *I beseech guidance, damn it.*

20A: Dreamed I was eating mango at the bottom of a ship. The sea was rocking it. Wish I could remember the rest. Was scared for my hair . . .

Rebuking in the name of the Lord.

20A: I screamed and it woke me.

[*Remember the ghost girl who laughed? Never could quite put my finger on it, but I swear, there was something like running feet inside that laugh.*]

Y: Such dreams come from a far country. Wish I could remember mine.

20A: You don't have to remember a dream to benefit from it.

It is three hours before the help arrives. By then, the wind has lessened; everyone files outside into the now-dark, everyone except the cuss-and-pray lady and the woman with the two children—the little one still fussing, the other sucking his thumb. Yolanda gives 20A half a stick of gum; it is peppermint and sweet. They chew quietly and watch the hound with its legs outstretched. The guitar guy unlatches his case and the dead moths blow out with the wind; they fill the sky like bits of worry paper. Yolanda catches one, peers at it in her cupped palms, then opens her hands and watches it ride the air. Later when it's time to reboard, 20A and Yolanda take the same seats as before—two rows behind the bus driver. The bus is quiet, all except for the cuss-and-pray lady who is humming—a funny hum that sounds like grace and dust devil.

Y: I was only six. The water rose to my armpits.

Yolanda writes furiously in 20A's notebook. Her pen moves across the page as turbulently as the Rio Grande did that day when she crossed. There were three of them. She was the little one. Her brother, Bembe was thirteen; her cousin, Naldo, fourteen. Bembe, hoisted her around his waist, her feet skimming the raging current. Naldo led the way over the slippery rocks—Bembe stepping where Naldo stepped and Yolanda holding on tight, her arms around her brother's neck.

A woman behind them yelled above the roar of the river, her words a language Yolanda did not know—but which she understood—desperation being the same no matter the tongue. Her hand reached out for Yolanda's feet, and Yolanda still clinging to her brother, extended her left leg—as far as it could go. The woman grasped the little ankle, trying to steady herself in the water, Yolanda's shoe falling and spinning downriver. And so it was, the four crossed the "Rio Bravo;" Yolanda's cousin before; she, on her brother's back; a stranger holding her foot. The water was fast and no-nonsense, having journeyed gorge and mountain, eager now to find its way to the delta, and to the open sea, turtles and shore birds awaiting.

As the four neared the middle, no one expected the surge of current which suddenly came. The river bustled them about, Naldo and Bembe struggling to stay upright. The water rose as Yolanda held on; her tired leg raised and extended—as far, far out as she could—she squeezed her eyes shut as the woman screaming, lost grasp of her toe—

Y: You are the only person I've ever told.

20A: The bus is limbo. Stories are safe.

167

HURRICANE EFFECT

there is a place 20A never goes in her dreams—

the place of flightless birds. The caracara walk along the coast, searching for crabs. Their legs long and strong, they walk the walk of birds who have made peace with their flightlessness. The sea laps rhythmic and slow—in no haste for the future already-come. Few dreamers come here; this no-name isle, so balm and ownself and quiet-mind.

The caracara reminisce fondly of cane trash in a boy's hair; burrow their beaks deep in the sand. The older ones argue amongst themselves whether it was dream, memory, or imagination which brought him there—which one? There is a flurry of sand and feather. They beak-bicker above the beach until one of the younger ones says, All of it; none of it. What it matter, eh? He got here. He learned to bend the air. Yes, the old ones say. He found us, fi true. He learned to bend the air.

zachariah: wind & fiah

During the calm of the storm's eye, the silver-hair man has rescued his two goats from the verandah and tended the chicks, the hen now roosting in a box in the kitchen. Cement blocks are set on the zinc roof; and a just-in-case pan in the middle of the room is ready for leaks. Having eaten the last of his tin mackerel and cleaned the plate with a piece of breadfruit, silver-hair returns to bed to ride out the worst. If the roof blow and tings dread, at least mi belly full, he says out loud; and a brown wall-lizard turns its head, feeling into the bass in his words.

All night, the wind makes wheezing sounds against the window, and the man dreams he is the driver of an old country bus with goats and noisy chickens and baskets overfull of banana and yellow yam and dasheen, and look, *one* soon-ripe No. 11 mango. The bus has fifty-five seats and each seat is occupied by the same-same person—a young woman with long braids and a backpack on her lap. The young miss has her eyes closed and sings a song, "Eleven times eleven." A sweet reggae tune, sweet like festival. As the man drives, he hums the song too, and finds that as he hums, the miss multiplies and the bus becomes longer and longer, each seat occupied by her and her new moon face.

Outside, the hurricane roars along. Near midnight, the box in the kitchen tips over and the hen and chicks cluck-cluck around the house, find their way under the breathing bed. Hurricane rain pounds the roof the way horses gallop the dreamiverse. The horses follow a spiral racecourse, and as they turn and turn again, a name comes to the sleeping man—Zachariah. In the dream the name is familiar and he repeats it and repeats it until he realises, but wait—is his own name—*fi true,* he says out loud, startling the chicks, and the dream stops and restarts, and Abba appears.

She is holding a wristwatch to her ear, and shaking it, and shaking it, and he finds that he knows what she is thinking. She thinks she hears baby-cry inside the watch; he feels her pain-o-heart, thinks maybe he hears it too—a far-far cry—ancient and just-now. Yes, this cane trash sound is what storms are made of; what sorrow-wail is made of. Abba catches a glimpse of him and spins around, shoves the watch in her pocket.

I come to leap with you, he says—

DIS ALGORIDDIM; OR,

out of the blak and blue

20A: What is the jahlixir made of?

DREAMGATE DREAD: An open secret

20A: But what is the jahlixir made of?

DREAMGATE DREAD: Chant-it-again

20A: Just tell me, nuh. What is the jahlixir made of?

DREAMGATE DREAD: Is cannabis dis

20A: No joke Ras, what is the jahlixir made of?

DREAMGATE DREAD: Big chune, dawta. Big chune.

20A: Is it real?

DREAMGATE DREAD: What is real?

her dream membrane [duppy wallpaper]4.

Look-here, bits of flight from Wednesday evening   radio show;

riffs of tunes from under *on formed against this house*

shall prosper.

side a croton leaf

keep the record on migration & left-

over   talk;   the machine will grind you to dust; don't let it;   remember

that

time one asked you

No weapon formed against this house shall prosper.

for your passport?

hello? you're on the air.   Taino sistah: *They lied. We're*

it is strongly suspected, birds fly from port

to port

gastropods are asymmetrical;

176

20A nods off again. Yolanda Moreno next to her, is also (finally) dreaming. There is spittle at one corner of her mouth and in her dream she revises the story she confided earlier about wading across the Rio Grande to cross the border. In her dream, she flies instead. Her eyes flicker-flicker when she dreams this part, and the greyhound pushes through darkness. 20A sees Yolanda's wings like black words on a white page and she notes in her notebook that the act of dreaming likes to be in present tense. But she is only vaguely aware of Yolanda and of her fly story now because she is dream-watching the man from the-already call out to Abba—

[*Exit*]

Meanwhile, Yolanda next to her rises above an Arizona dust haze; she heads east, backtracking towards Texas, cruising low over Louisiana, Mississippi, and the long nose of Florida, and finally, taking off across the shimmering Caribbean. She holds a very old book against her chest, and has painted her nails amarillo; there are wings twain her elbows, and wings twain her ankles—she flies in reverse the way dragonflies do, along the curved arm of Cuba, offering libation to Havana before dipping down to Jamaica and skimming the Palisadoes to Port Royal; she skirts the scattered islands of the Antilles; cuts a bend around Trinidad, flying backways to the coast where Guyana meets Venezuela, flaunting a fly style that can only come after nights of sleeplessness; Colombia, Panama, Costa Rica, Honduras, Guatemala, Belize; the herstory of their names takes her breath away; from high above, she views starfish and anemone and stingrays and crabs and miles and miles of kelp and coral reef, some of it eroding; she charts full passage around the bowl of the gulf then cuts across Mexico, all the way back to the brown roar water of the Rio Grande, the place she crossed when she was six.

[*Exit*]

[*Exit*]

The highway is dark; the driver sips coffee. 20A leans into the dream membrane. There are voices moving in and out; and running feet; and dancing; and drum-and-chant; bits of *what if?* float there; machete stab caught in it, too; and lover's rock; and leaf of life; and hallelujah tongues. There, in the warm betwixt and between, 20A thinks to herself, what if she could dream-cut a path to Yolanda? A child a few seats back drops a plastic wind-up toy. It rolls down the aisle and lodges behind the driver, still moving its tail

as from high up above, Yolanda sees a woman in the water; she is waving and calling over the river rush, something familiar in the frenzy of her arms. Yolanda makes an arc and swoops a little lower, her amarillo toes skimming the quick water. She reaches for the woman's hand—their fingers nearly touching; and all the while, people watch from both sides of the riverbank: they are Mexico and Nicaragua and Colombia and Peru and Venezuela and Guatemala and Ecuador and Brazil and Honduras and El Salvador and Guyana and Belize. Some have crossed sea to arrive there too: Cuba and Haiti and Jamaica and Congo and Cameroon and Ghana and India and China and Turkey, too many to name—past and future held in their breath. Undeterred by the wind pressing her wings and tossing her hair, Yolanda flies as close as she can. She peers into the woman's face—wet with river and mud and journey—and sees: the eyes of 20A, dreaming back at her.

For in her dream, 20A has revised the story told earlier about arriving at Newark. In this dream, she visits Vee in Panama instead and has made the long and treacherous journey to the Mexican/US border—

Someone's hat floats by. And a cellphone case. And a styrofoam cup. 20A fights to steady herself in the water. Yolanda caught up in wind, likewise, struggles to stay aloft; she flies off upstream, then swoops back in again, stretching an arm—as far as it can go—still, their hands miss.

You're dreaming, 20A yells to her above the roar of the river, *You did it!*

178

I knew I'd remember you! Yolanda calls as she flies upstream again, hair and tears streaming behind her, her wings flapping fast-fast. *I never forgot you.* At a bend in the river she makes a u-turn and dives for 20A but the river is quick and 20A is swept from her reach. The people watching suck in their breath; the water is nearly to 20A's chest; they see that there is not much time.

You did it! 20A shouts, unfazed by the rising river. And she notes that, there in the middle of the Rio Grande, they are speaking to each other—out loud.

In the mixed frequency of dream, memory and imagination, Yolanda and 20A call across spaces and times; across languages and herstories; across lost seasons. Mexico and Nicaragua and Colombia and Peru and Venezuela and Guatemala and Ecuador and Brazil and Honduras and El Salvador and Guyana and Belize and Cuba and Haiti and Jamaica and Congo and Cameroon and Ghana and India and China and Turkey, and too many to name—hear, each in a different beat, and in accordance with their own longings. They watch from the banks, still holding their breath—

Black birds, too, watch; their feet grip barbed wire lining the bank. This time, Yolanda reaches with the book—it is heavy and slick in her hands. *See if these grow where you are going!* she calls, her tears longer than all the miles of the people.

What the rah, you did it, 20A says again, and her words ring out through the dream membrane and fill the jahlixir, every space of it, into I-finity. The water is nearly up to her neck; she can't stand much longer. Yolanda almost out of strength, inhales deep and swoops in one last time—the people can hardly bear it—*Ahora!* someone yells. And the birds open their noisy-noisy beaks; and 20A lurches for the book; and the pages flutter in the wind before the book hits the water and swirls, dancing downstream, tiny seeds scattered—

20A //wakes up to desert scrub. Yolanda is still sleeping. Her eyelids flick-flicker. Her mouth twitches.

At Flagstaff, they both get off the bus.

I'll miss you, Yolanda says out loud. Except in dream, it is only the second time 20A has heard her voice. It has river stones in it. And fossils from deep sea-bottom. Yolanda is leaving to catch the bus to LA. Bembe is somewhere there; she wants to find him; and find a job. She will save money to go to school, to study the lineage of very old insects, and Spanish too, perhaps—having almost forgotten it.

Maybe you'll become famous, 20A says.

Yolanda smiles and the praying mantis above her lip moves a little. The guitar guy walks by and disappears down the road.

mango-time: *girls on swings under trees on the dubside of the I-niverse*
[arkive audio/119]

what the rah, you did it; just-so/just-so; just-so/just-so; just-so/just-so; just-so/
just-so; ∿ …just-so/just-so; just-so/just-so; just-so/just-so; just-so/just-so;
just-so/just-so; just-so/just-so; just-so/just-so; just-so/just-so; just-so/just-so;
just-so/just-so; just-so/just-so; just-so/just-so; just-so/just-so; just-so/just-so;
just-so/just-so; just-so/just-so; just-so/just-so; just-so/just-so; just-so/just-so;
just-so/just-so; what the rah, you did it; just-so/just-so; just-so/just-so; just-so/
just-so; just-so/just-so; just-so/just-so; just-so/just-so; just-so/just-so; just-so/
just-so; just-so/just-so; just-so/just-so; just-so/just-so; just-so/just-so; just-so/
just-so; just-so/just-so; ∿ … just-so/just-so; just-so/just-so; just-so/just-so;
just-so/just-so; just-so/just-so; just-so/just-so;just-so/just-so; just-so/just-so;
just-so/just-so; just-so/just-so; what the rah, you did it; just-so/just-so;just-so/
just-so; just-so/just-so; just-so/just-so; just-so/just-so; just-so/just-so; just-so/
just-so; just-so/just-so; just-so/just-so; just-so/just-so; just-so/just-so; just-so/
just-so; just-so/just-so; just-so/just-so; just-so/just-so; just-so/just-so; just-so/
just-so; just-so/just-so; just-so/just-so; just-so/just-so; just-so/just-so; just-so/
just-so; just-so/just-so; just-so/just-so; ∿ … what the rah, you did it;
just-so/just-so;just-so/just-so; just-so/just-so; just-so/just-so; just-so/just-so;
just-so/just-so; just-so/just-so; just-so/just-so; just-so/just-so; just-so/just-so;
just-so/just-so; just-so/just-so; just-so/just-so; just-so/just-so; ∿ …just-so/
just-so; just-so/just-so; just-so/just-so; just-so/just-so; just-so/just-so; just-so/
just-so; just-so/just-so; just-so/just-so; just-so/just-so;just-so/just-so; what the
rah, you did it; just-so/just-so; just-so/just-so; just-so/just-so; just-so/just-so;
just-so/just-so; just-so/just-so; just-so/just-so; just-so/just-so; just-so/just-so;
just-so/just-so; just-so/just-so; just-so/just-so; just-so/just-so; just-so/just-so;
just-so/just-so; just-so/just-so; just-so/just-so; just-so/just-so; just-so/just-so;
just-so/just-so; just-so/just-so;just-so/just-so;just-so/just-so; what the rah, you
did it; just-so/just-so; just-so/just-so; just-so/just-so; just-so/just-so; just-so/
just-so; just-so/just-so; just-so/just-so; just-so/just-so;

DIVINE RETROGRADE

Abba; *nuff wheel* [Arkive Audio Transcript/6]

there he is—the silver-strange man—he holds
my hand, tight & sure-sure. strange ting to have mi hand inside the skin
of another, no one ever do me this. only
Quaco, baby-sweet—he squeezed my
finger while he suck mi no-milk tit. but
this man have time-&-neva in his palm, like he come from a

wheelin. he lay a stick cross the ground & say, when i count all the way
to
          I-finity, jump quick.
I-finity? i say. i don't know that one—i don't learn all mi numbers-dem
yet. & he laugh & say, you know that one—it same age as you.

madam fate flowers turnin, turnin in his two eyes & the petals-dem
          multicate & multicate—
& his hand warm & ting, &
          the ground rot & not
steady under mi
          feet & mi feel mi-self a young & new come-again ting—all
                    moonshine & antidote seed-drum
wing & cocoon whiss ting &
the man neigh—like a horse mi did know—
eh?
& then mi hear it clear-clear: dogs barking in a far-far woodland & mi
tink: what if mi baby Quaco on the other
          side? &
mi jump—

[cough]; also, ewa; also, ikó; also, u̱kwarà; also, kosuk; also, ketiketoo; also—

The bell rings at Port Royal and Adwoa coughs #3,206—this one to wake the baby which still breathes, a descendant calling, calling its name. They shuffle them up to the deck—the 191 who remain. Ashante woman's knees are weak; her legs shake; her head spins. But, there is air. Yes, there is air. Someone slaps her cheeks; pours water over her head. Later, they line them up—the 191—in rows on the sandy beach. Hermit crabs scurry their feet; iguanas watch, curious from a distance. And a wind from the past moves upon Ashante woman's left; and a wind from the yet-to-come moves upon her right; and she stands, and holds her head, and sets her face, all roots and modda-land strong, and does not fall.

where she landed;

You know those country women you see walking by the side of the road? Drive carefully. Some of them are madam fate flowers; some of them are snails; some of them are cannabis duppy gal. They are always there. They might be your mother, or your sister, or your best friend—arrived from far, without chick or chile.

It was sometime after hurricane Gilbert clean-up, that someone noticed what looked to be an unusual plant growing at a bend of a St. Thomas road—the leaves dark green and waxy and with tendrils which curled from nodes along the edges. People said the tendrils looked like curly lashes around an open eye, the leaves opening and closing in reaction to sound and silence. When babies laughed the leaves were observed to stretch wide open, and at night they closed shut and wept a clear liquid. A local botanist suggested it might be a species come back from extinction. He roped off the area with plans to take samples, consult with colleagues at the university in town; but later, returned with his collection bag, the plant was gone—soldier ants scurried in its place; there were no signs of uproot. This female plant [item 146] was never identified. In the arkive it exists as *where she landed* and can now only be viewed by Shante dreamers,* or otherwise by fugitives walking the backside of the veil. On occasion, *where she landed* twines the trunks of silk cotton trees and is visible to betwixt and between ones deep in sweet medidread. A leaf of this plant chewed seventy times seven is an antidote to insomnia.

Of Shante Dreamers

Couba Cornwallis; also, Cubah; also, Cuba; b. ?–1848?

There is a long line of powerful Shante dreamers in Jamaica. Named and unnamed, they inhabit the arkive. If, while visiting, you experience a whirling at the base of your spine, it is likely one of the long-time inhabitants—they move that way. Couba Cornwallis, the gifted obeah woman, herbalist, healer and another high priestess of the Unmarked Grave Club of Women Geniuses, is most certainly one of them and would have been familiar with 146. She is the name sake of Quaco; also, Cuba; also, Cue boy. According to arkival records, Couba and Quaco crossed paths once, he arrived in Port Royal at her doorstep, running from history; searching for herstory. She was sweeping the stoop and took one look at the feather/eggshell/last-laugh knot bag in his hand and said, Keep going.

20A stands alone outside the bus station. With the exception of the cuss-and-pray woman, everyone has departed. She scans the street for neckties. Cuss-and-pray is at the ticket desk demanding a refund; the bus was delayed, she argues, and now she has missed her connection and won't get to her grandson's wedding in San Diego; Jesus help, damn it.

Uncertain what to do next, 20A sits inside by the revolving door. There's a brochure for a tour bus to the Grand Canyon; it leaves from the station and there's a coupon too. If she withdraws the money for her electric bill, she can go. Cuss-and-pray sits on a bench eating an orange, all amazing grace and shit. Her socks are rolled down and the laces of one shoe are undone. She and 20A sit on opposite sides of the room but keep each other company, in some sort of way. Cuss-and-pray glances up each time 20A unzips her backpack or digs in her pockets; she dirty-looks the desk clerks and their holy bull shit on 20A's behalf. 20A feels a little sad when the tour bus comes.

sista kurata plays that one again

For days, you have been hearing a far-off wail, a sound riding the jahlixir. Still, you have planted your spirit garden and washed your rootswoman t-shirt and written a letter and gone to the post office and come back and taken the already-dry off the line and visited a fever neighbour and administered cerasee and bay leaf and argued with the lizards and cut the pumpkin, carrot and cho cho for soup, and kneaded love dumplings—all without haste, but before noon. According to studies, at sea-level time unfolds slower. In the arklve both sea-level and the colour yellow bend time. It is mango season and you stand in your doorway, contemplating a number 11—yellow and flat on both sides. In both dream and wide-awake, horses love to eat mangoes; you love this about them—it makes them kin—and soothes wail. There are many shades of yellow on this island, the yellow of mango on a muzzle being one of them. From April poui flowers to baby jaundice, you collect all of it. Bits of yellow eggshell dot the arkive like shards of memory, seeking balm. Is what that sound?

At the Grand Canyon 20A stands with her face to the wind; if the wind has something to say, then she wants to hear it. There is a big coach with overseas tourists nearby. The wind blows her braids; bits of yellow-red dust settle on her skin. 20A remembers hearing this story: a man and a woman met here, perhaps just a few yards from where she is standing. It is said, the charge of the grand fissure was so strong, it had pulled them to its edge, made their eyes lock. The woman was running from some sadness; she had written her sorrow on lined paper and torn it to pieces, and come to the canyon to breathe, and throw the bits away. The canyon is big enough to swallow such things. The man had come for the raw landscape of America; and then he saw the woman, and the concealment of something in her smile. He took her photo and the click of the lens changed their paths; and they got married. 20A likes this story because the woman, a fugitive from cares-of-life, found solace, and outran sorrow.

20A feels a lump in her throat. She wants to cry like Yolanda, but will not let herself. Instead, she screams her name into the red raw of the canyon. The tourists pretend not to notice; they zip up their jackets and take more pictures and get back inside the coach. 20A's voice skitter-scatters over rock like the woman's bits of worry paper.

20A thinks: She could hide in this place. Sleep in a crook under a boulder. Eat leftovers from the visitor center garbage. Drink from the Colorado River at the bottom of the canyon. Find a cave to shield from the wind. By the time they found her, she would have grown fur, mated with a coyote and become a naturalized citizen.

20A thinks: She could also go home.

azureceruleanindigoinksapphirecobaltnewmoonblueazureceruleanindigo
inksapphirecobaltnewmoonblueazureceruleanindigoinksapphirecobaltnew
*moon*drinksbox*blueazureceruleanindigoinksapphirecobaltnewmoon*
blueazureceruleanindigoinksapphirecobaltperiwinkleblueazureceruleanindigo
*inksapphirecobaltnewmoon*bottleglass*blueazure . . . it should/be no/surprise/*
that the bell/of the/henrietta/marie/reappeared/at sea-bottom/centuries later,
1983./shante woman/had a/way about her . . . ceruleanindigoinksapphire
*cobaltnewmoon*sodacan*blueazureceruleanindigoinksapphirecobaltnew*
*moonblueazureceruleanindigoinksapphirecobalnewmoon*scandalbag
blueazureceruleanindigoinksapphirecobaltnewmoonblueazureceruleanindigo
inksapphirecobaltnewmoonblu—

Cuba has been listening to the stars from under the kindah tree. It is the summer of Finsler's comet—a streak of bright light brushing the handle of the Big Dipper. The girl, and Ms. Z. and the one they call Colonel, are all gone to bed.

Somewhere underneath the star-hum, he is aware of his wail, all echo and reverb. The stars trance and soothe, just-so, and he feels in his pocket for the knot-cloth, comforted that it is still there. The cloth smells of earth and nest; and a bless-ting whirls in it and perseverance beats in it. There under the Bombay kindah, he thinks to himself, that he will keep going, for what is there to lose? Perhaps, one day fi-true, he will find the mill girl again, and her loveful eyes; he'll know it's her because she'll stop time. Or perhaps one day fi-true, he will find his modda again—the whole trail of them—for story has it, he was a found-chile and had many; their voices, just-so/just-so—

butterfly, please don't cry

Gramma has dozed off on the verandah, her hand in her pocket clutching the last bit of nutmeg. In her half-dream, the garden grows wild and first-time—the way it was before construction came; before Kingston came; before the ships on the horizon came. And in the place where she sits, there grows a great mahoe tree. Its trunk is tall and proud and its flowers blink yellow, then red; yellow, then red.

Just when she discerns that she is a swallowtail and can pitch and rest unseen on the bark of the tree, a brown dog at the gate barks for crackers, and she stirs. Gramma searches her bag, but the crackers are all finished. The little dog leaves, lies down by the curb; and Gramma watches the hills, her sock feet on the tile floor. Duck ants dig tunnels beneath where her soles rest; there, under the base of the house—for yes, they *can travel a mile or more.* In the absence of the mahoe and ebony and pimento and bitterwood that once filled the Liguanea plain, they have come to eat her house instead. In the mornings, she sees their little wings on the floor and sweeps them up, wonders how far out their tunnel goes. She pictures them burrowing from yard to yard, eating down Kingston. The wings appear and reappear throughout the day—there is no end to sweeping them.

Dark comes, and a deep bass on night-skye speakahs fills the street. Gramma looks out the window to see if her grans come back from party yet—

> *good god almighty, is late now and the people's music big-so and the sea at Hellshire rising up, rising up—our mother covers her nakedness with raiment.*

SAME RIDDIM, DIFFERENT CHUNE

 He finds himself at Half Way Tree square, wheeled there on the curved riff of his own wail. It is Kingston-hot and he is carrying a backpack full of sand and ca-racara feathers. He feels oddly at home. No one—except for the aperture of a camera across the street—sees him. There are people boarding a minibus to country and he follows behind them and boards too; a voice sings deliverance songs on the radio, and an old woman pinches him and asks, What yu name? Cuba, he says, without even thinking. And the woman throws back her head with laugh, her mouth opening wide-wide like a beak. Nah, she says, leaning closer to his ear. I go call you Cue Boy. Look how you arrive—right here-so, just on time. And she throws back her head again and laughs some more. Cue Boy looks down at his new shoes feet, not sure what to do. The old woman wipes sky wata from her eyes, pulls a bus fare from her bosom, puts it in his hand-middle, then steps off the bus.

He rides it all the way to country. There is riddim and cuss-cuss on it, and ripe june-plum smell and dread youth and school girl and babycry. The bus cuts the curves of the hill and gully road, tilting sideways at the same angle the earth tilts as it rides the kosmos, and the people talk scandal bag/ and sensimilla/ and belly laugh/ and dutty tough/ and guinea hen weed/ and bloodfiah/ and look-here: dis one-stop/ and rise-up/ and chant it/ to rhaatid—Cue Boy likes that last one best, and vows to use it.

hear him?

He gets off the bus at Port Antonio, the street busy with Friday market and school let-out and rah-rah and palangpang. A rollaway mango rests near a gutter and Cue Boy picks it up and bites into it. He sucks on the seed and follows the sea road all the way to Folly where it begins to rain and a woman and a small two-plaits girl stands waiting under an umbrella. *Wata more than flour,* the woman says to herself, and Cue Boy hearing the worry in her words, stops to listen. *More than sugar too,* she whispers to the air, and Cue Boy replies, Yes Mam, but wi nah give up. The woman looks left and right, over both shoulders, *Wha?* And the girl, catching a strange remembrance, puts her hand over her mouth and smiles.

Cue Boy walks until it is night, the road lit up with headlights and now-and-then fireflies. He stops to rest at a rocky cove, stretches his body alongside the shore, feeling riddim in the ground from a bar down the road. Hermit crabs crawl over his shoulders, nestle in his armpits; some enter his dreams.

In the morning, there is a lost American across the street. She has a shock of red hair and long legs in velvet leggings; winter flight in her voice—*ello? I'm near Boston Bay . . . hello? we got disconn . . . hello?*

Hearing sparrows caught up in syllables, Cue Boy draws closer. *What was I thinking wearing velvet*—Ms. swoops up her bags, waves down a white taxi; and Cue Boy watches as the car drives away, her sea shawl caught in the shut door.

He is still standing there watching the shawl when an old pelican, come in from sea, lands next to him, drinks rain from a pan left under an almond tree. Cue Boy drinks too, then continues walking, the street soon busy with buses and radio chune and baby moddahs and hungry dogs and dreadah-dan-dread.

axial tilt;

Near Manchioneal, he veers off the road, walks and walks and finds himself in woodland bush, green moss breathing in, and out. Away from the dust and the trucks and the kiss-mi-rass cuss, it is quiet there. Insects mind their own business and antidote seeds rest, knowing they can live forever. Birds preen and watch; a stream runs through it. He walks until it is just-so. A woman deep in spliff under a tree observes Cue Boy approaching from the other side of her smoke; the forest so wake-up and livity in the haze. Bless, she says softly as Cue Boy draws near, and she offers him her spliff. Cue Boy pauses, her smoke filling his head. She smiles—her eyes swirling with stars, cinnamon and brown sugar—and pats the ground. Come, she says. And she draws in the spliff and passes/ it and he sits next to her and puffs/ it and passes/ as if he and the woman and the wisdom/ weed have known each other since before/ time—

She wears only one shoe—the barefoot scratch and swell—but, so calmify and neva mind she is; her gaze following the trees, feeling the green. A stick insect makes its way up Cue Boy's arm; moss burrows between her toes. They smoke in silence and watch the canopy of leaves, see how there is a wheelin in it.

After a while and a while and a while, perceiving that here—at last—is a person who might understand, Cue Boy says all sof, Mi run with the birds. And mi hear the stars-them hum.

At the sound of his voice, the woman turns. And looks at him. Touches his eyelids. Opens his hand-middle. Searches the lines there. Knocks on his knees.

Oi?

Then, she holds him. Oi, she holds him; just-so/just-so.

And she cries. She sobs through lifetimes, it seems. The woods all wet and moddahstrong. Her riva coming down, coming down; all sipple rock and leap of heart. Oi, mi cane-whip chile.

At the end of it, she wipes her face with the hem of her scarf, then wipes his. For she sees—that yes, is him, is her one-chile, and yes, he knows—her wood-smoke smell; the centuries in her eyes, turnin, turnin. Baby can remember far-far like that?

His knowing goes away, soon as it comes. *Oi?* Then returns—quick as

drop-down mango. Yes-yes, fi true, he knows her—and she busts out laughing, and he does too. They shut their eyes—to better see—and laugh through lifetimes again: in and out of star chant; the algoriddims of dreams; the sound entangled in chi-chi bud call; the Grandie Nanny smell of damp earth and that feeling you get when a DJ spin it right. For don't is this life is made of? Seasons of laugh, and of Quaco-cry?

When Cue Boy opens his eyes again,

huh? Moddah is gone. Only a bush there. It has leaf-lids and tendrils like curly lashes, a clear liquid seeping. A slender stem reaches—far, far as it can—and coils his finger—

oi, mi lost & found.

Cue Boy feels a—

stir the air. A no name ting. Because the love a mother has for her child bears no language; occupies all time and all space, is without beginning and without end, and is strong enough to bring wilderness back from extinction.

The no name touches the side of his face—oi, cane-whip chile—brushes centuries-old mill dust from his cheekbone; oi, deliverance;

as the long-dead, and the not-yet born, and the invisible ones watching from the now-dark, rise up; oi, heartmake.

Mama? calls a girl from a far-far place.

Rhaatid, Cue Boy says, sof-sof.

WAKE THE TOWN,
AND TELL THE PEOPLE

remix comin thru the speakahs; or, waxing gibbous & redreaming after
bed on a bus; or, 20A's return dream

She lands in Half Way Tree square. It is early morning and quiet. Across
the road, a man is pushing on the door to a clocktower. Something is
familiar—like she read this half-open door in a book—all bass and roots
and dreadfullness.

"Is a book this?" she calls, "Me in a dream book? A dread-dream?"

"Is only *one* book there is," the man says, "and yes, you in it."

"Rah," she says, all sof and don't-believe.

hey, can you hear that? [arkive sample]

Tuff meets 20A at the airport. Back from America with her one-suitcase
and horseshoe and old braids, she is not sure what to expect. She sees
Tuff before he sees her—he is still lanky but with little dreads coming
up, and a beard too. She waves and his smile lights her up—he has always been her comrade in tribulation. She is back—without chick or
chile—and feels no shame.

They drive down Palisadoes with the window open and a warm breeze on
their face. Tuff turns on the radio—the tail end of a woman's laugh before
the news cuts in with St. Thomas flood and missing children and murder
she wrote. Near Rockfort, a cargo ship is docked in harbour, in conspiracy
with steal-away youth; a monk seal hums incognito. A voice on the radio
says *a suh wi dweet* and someone laughs again and then a jingle cuts in, to
try dis ting. You think I could be a DJ? 20A asks—then puts her hand over
her mouth—having never had that thought before. *Sea-level rising; Hell-*
shire beach soon gone, the radio says. She feels a little light-headed, maybe
it's the heat; or maybe it's the mashup riddims on the radio; or the dead
dog by the side of the road; or the smell of overripe mango. You'll need
a new name, Tuff says. And they brainstorm names—Flygyal, Krucial,
Sistrenz, Akoustic, She-Riddim, Zempress—all the way down Windward
Road and onto Mountainview Ave. Orange love bush climbs a fence; there

is a whiff of grief as they pass a man at a bus stop; the cable wires carry politricks and badmind, but underneath that, bless–up and uprise. At the next light, the road veers left, just-so—

Near Crossroads 20A has a thought that she could return the Ms. Z. book. Tuff doesn't work at the bookstore anymore but she still could, nuh? For truth is, she didn't win the book for best essay at all, but rather, thought she should have, so borrowed it instead. She looks out the window and decides that she will take it back next week; that this will be a way of pressing her reset button; spinning back time.

Tuff navigates traffic, routing and rerouting to avoid evening rush. He knows Kingston better than the lines in his hand-middle, taking back roads and gully passes; cutting passed yards with ackee and jimbilin and coral vine. 20A loses track of where they really are, but at some point they emerge onto Maxfield Ave. Near Hagley Park, amid a glory of electric poles, black wires, buses and after-work fuss, there is a youth standing in the middle of the street. He seems unaware that he is holding up traffic. He is looking at the sky, watching a flock of birds overhead. Cars honk; people on the sidewalk jeer; a school boy throws a box drink. Still, he does not move.

Soon, the people, too, watch the flock—sky-skanking over Kingston. The birds-them rejoice; and they rebuke and warn. Such a screeching and cawing of things not seen. Check it. Such a dip and dance of it; a knowing that the air is enough. 20A sticks her head out the window and calls, How far them coming from? The youth looks towards the sound of her voice—*something mill and cane trash in it; something mill and cane trash in it*—then back at the flock. The birds go, A suh wi dweet/a suh wi dweet/a suh wi dweet/ over the riddim on the radio. And Kingston stops for a full minute as the people notice the wi-finity of the sky and of the way their feet no longer touch ground; and how—but-wait—the ackee tree chants them, and they chant it. They ponder the arkitekture of evening light and feel something ancient and rise-up inside them. The woman about to honk her horn decides she will go home now and plant bromeliads beneath her window; a youth decides to seek Jah light; babymothers waiting in line for under-wage realise they are queens to rass; Tuff, with far-eye, sees inside the knot-cloth fallen in the street; and 20A discerns her DJ name.

Big-up yu-self, the people call to each other, for the first time understanding the true power of these words. Later those who remember the long minute, remember it only as a dream, but are never the same.

WATCH THIS:

The caracara will be pleased when the youth returns. He will appear on the shore, wet and muddy, having wheeled there from time-until. He will have a faint smile on his face, weathered and long-journey. The caracara will peck-peck all around him; pick cane trash and mango blossom from his hair.

The old ones will argue whether he is chile or man—which one? The young ones will kick the sand; peck at the knotted cloth in his palm, curious about the crunch of feather and egg shell. *Xenothrix* monkeys will watch from the trees.

It will be sun-hot on the little no-name island, the sky a still and cloudless blue. The caracara will be surprised when the wind comes—the boy's eyes suddenly open, his smile growing. They will be even more surprised when he laughs, having never heard bass sound system before.

Quaco laugh will reverb across time and time-again/ Queen Nanny will hear it and assemble her army/ lost geese will hear it and suddenly change course/ it will catch in the echo of a dub tune on a radio/ in a dog's broken bark/ in a riff of dreaming yard; bromeliads blooming/ the *heh-heh* of a woman come back from the dead/ school children will hear it and run to the window to look/ someone will remember the *boss* in *simply boss*/ a baby will speak in the womb, *what the rah?*/Kingston mangoes will ripe before season—

BUT WHEEL IT UP, FOR

Hellshire good as gone; and 20A is anxious now to get to her Gramma's house. A warm wind coming down from the hills stirs up trash as a girl runs to catch a flyway page from a book; she sits on a wall to read it, her fingers tracing words on the paper. 20A has an odd feeling that she is watching herself; or, that she is watching herself watch herself; and too, that all this has happened before. The sun goes down behind concrete; traffic moves slow and crawl-pon-belly. Two goats bleat down Babylon and buck their horns—*the cane in hurricane.* The light turns red and a man selling pineapple knocks on the window. 20A shakes her head. Seek and find, hear? he says.

This Kingston makes her head spin; makes her in love with it and at war with it; makes her all bloodfiah and spirit anthem. They drive over a woman's shoe in the road; a radio voice says, *Catch this*—

At Gramma's house, Tuff helps her with her suitcase; he'll call tomorrow, he says. He's nice that way. She wonders what kinda righteous bam bam they will get up to now. He waits for her to close the gate, beeps his horn, then leaves. A little dog watches from across the street.

mango-time: *girls on swings under trees in a spirit yard near Andromeda*
[arkive audio/92]

*just-so/just-so/***&*** just-so/just-so/just-so/just-so/just-so/just-so/just-so/*∿*just-so/*
just-so/just-so/just-so/just-so/just-so/just-so/just-so/just-so/just-so/just-so/just-so/
just-so/just-so/just-so/just-so/just-so/just-so/just-so/just-so/just-so/just-so/just-so/
just-so/just-so/just-so/just-so/just-so/just-so/just-so/just-so/just-so/just-so/just-so/
just-so/just-so/just-so/just-so/just-so/just-so/just-so/just-so/just-so/just-so/just-so/
*just-so/just-so/just-so/just-so/just-so/just-so/just-so/**just-so/just-so/just-so/***
just-so/just-so/just-so/just-so/just-so/just-so/just-so/just-so/just-so/just-so/
just-so/just-so/just-so/just-so/just-so/just-so/just-so/just-so/just-so/just-so/
just-so/just-so/just-so/jusl-so/jusl-so/just-so/just-so/just-so/just-so/just-so/
just-so/just-so/just-so/just-so/just-so/ just-so/just-so/just-so/just-so/just-so/
just-so/just-so/just-so/just-so/just-so/just-so/just-so/ just-so/just-so/just-so/
just-so/just-so/just-so/just-so/just-so/just-so/just-so/just-so/ just-so/ just-so/
just-so/just-so/just-so/just-so/just-so/just-so/just-so/just-so/just-so/just-so/
just-so/just-so/just-so/just-so/just-so/just-so/just-so/just-so/just-so/just-so/
just-so/ just-so/just-so/just-so/just-so/just-so/just-so/just-so/just-so/just-so/
just-so/just-so/just-so/ just-so/just-so/just-so/just-so/just-so/just-so/just-so/
just-so/just-so/just-so/just-so/just-so/ just-so/just-so/just-so/just-so/just-so/
just-so/just-so/just-so/just-so/just-so/ just-so/just-so/just-so/ just-so/just-so/
just-so/just-so/just-so/just-so/just-so/just-so/just-so/just-so/just-so/ just-so/
just-so/just-so/just-so/just-so/just-so/just-so/just-so/just-so/just-so/just-so/just-so/
just-so/just-so/just-so/just-so/just-so/just-so/just-so/just-so/just-so/just-so/just-so/
*just-so/ just-so/***& you too, you know this/***just-so/just-so/just-so/just-so/just-so/*
*just-so/just-so/oi-oi*just-so/just-so/just-so/just-so/just-so/just-so/just-so/just-so/*
*∿*just-so/just-so/just-so/ just-so/just-so/just-so/just-so/just-so/just-so/just-so/*
*just-so/just-so/just-so/just-so/just-so/just-so/just-so/just-so/just-so/***for don't our
ancestors left algoriddims for our survival?***

214

NATURAL HERSTORY

she speaks & the stars hear her voice [arkive audio on night sky]

It's late but see me here, returned with mi eleven braids and one-suit-case, standing with mi back against the gate. Evening falls quick-quick. Look the sky—blue-already-turn-indigo. Pea doves murmur from a secret place. And oh-the-stars. Even in Kingston, they hum just-so/just-so. Mango leaves cover the concrete path, and the tree leans a little to the side. I thought the smell of No. 11 would make my mouth wata, but no, it's my eyes that well and wata.

Let me stand here little bit; pull myself together. The gate warms my back; sun and riddim still run in it. I had a dream once of a ting like this—I was standing before a neva-neva place and a man brought me every mango under the sun, except the one I really wanted—my soul mango. He said, That one, yu must find and grow inside yourself. And dreams being dreams, I looked out at neva-neva, all swirl and hum and come-again; and I said, How big is this place, Ras? And what it is made of? And he said, It's made of you; is you make it.

I am not one for remembering dreams, but I do remember that one. So see me here, in front Gramma's gate—and is me making this. Is me telling this. Did you know, our stories are endangered? I have returned to my own story without shame, for if there is any shame, it is only the shame of not having returned sooner.

Gramma? Gramma?

But Jesus, look how the verandah plants have grown up wild and ting, almost taking over the place; watch here—bougainvillea and bromeliads and bamboo palm and begonia and bird of paradise and dumb cane and cactus and croton and sinkle bible and a tall-tall snake plant; and look this, leaf-of-life in an old wash basin; fern and pink frangipani push from the outside and through the grill, eager for kinship.

Grams?

I almost don't see her through all the leaves—O Grams, waiting in a chair with her yellow-yellow house dress and socks and bed slippers. Gramma stretches a thin arm and I help her ease out the seat. We stand, quiet, in the already-dark; crickets, for once, hold their breath; a lizard tries to swallow a small stone. Grams rests her head in the crook of my neck—she smells of forest damp and flight paths and left-over wonda*; her heart goes badap badap—

Gramma? I say, my eyes welling up; and I cough a little cough—the way I remember she would do when she wanted to cry but needed to be brave.

Oi, mi chile, Gramma says, her heart racing. Hellshire gone and is mc-one, but I knew you would come. Quick, tell them everything—duck ants soon eat down the house, and there are no nutmegs left.

---

* **wonda**: *the kurata's preferred state of being and a necessary condition for full access to the arkive.*

OF ROOTS & FIAH
& SOUND-SISTREN CHANT

DREAMGATE DREAD: What is the jahlixir made of?

NIGHT-SKYE SPEAKAH: The algoriddims of black birds; the two ll's in ʌ∧ amarillo.

DREAMGATE DREAD: One more time from the top. What is the jahlixir made of?

NIGHT-SKYE SPEAKAH: *Simply boss,* Ras. Boss all through it.

DREAMGATE DREAD: Fi-true. But what is the jahlixir made of?

NIGHT-SKYE SPEAKAH: Turnin, turnin & far sound-sistren chant.

DREAMGATE DREAD: The lioness awakes. Come again, wheel it. What is the jahlixir made of?

NIGHT-SKYE SPEAKAH: The vibration of mango strings; quantum bass dreaming

DREAMGATE DREAD: Ah-oh. But tell me, what is the jahlixir made of?

NIGHT-SKYE SPEAKAH: A Gramma's long heart-wait. Oi. & seasons of cry. & of Quaco-laugh.

DREAMGATE DREAD: Ah, Empress. Is it real?

NIGHT-SKYE: What is real?

CATCH THIS —

There are places where Quaco-laugh has not yet arrived.
Light travels faster.
What ancient balm hurls towards us?

wooii,

skye

wooii,

a suh wi

dweet   a   suh wi dweet

wat

if?

w   at

if?

wat

i   f?

to Laurie Callahan, Barbara Epler, Mieke Chew and everyone at New Directions for believing in this book project. I am forever grateful. Thanks too, to Paul Sahre for the cover art.

Much gratitude for support from Creative Capital, the Whiting Foundation and the Eccles Institute at the British Library. This support has been vital and has helped make this book possible.

Michelle Herman, Kathy Fagan, Dr. Carole Boyce Davies, Eliot Weinberger, Indira Ganesan, Gang of Four and friends and colleagues at the University of Colorado Boulder and elsewhere, thank you for being a part of my journey.

Heart-bottom thanks to Laurent Fachon and Avani Fachon for their insight and for their love and support and for once again, being there for me. Bless-bless.

I am fortunate to have amazing siblings and family members. A million thanks to them.

Big up all the Jamaican musicians who are my soundtrack.

And gratitude and nuff respect to the women geniuses who have inspired and paved the way—Queen Nanny, Couba Cornwallis, Harriette Tubman, Zora Neale Hurston, Toni Morrison, Pamela Coleman Smith, Urselyn Johnson and Bernice Douglas. The Arkive is fueled by their greatness.

To the invisible ones who root for me, thank you.

Mama earth, I thank you. Jahlixir, I stand in wonda.